Dear Reader,

This month, celebrate Mother's Day with the best kind of treat four new love stories from Bouquet. Then again, *any* day is the right day to read romance....

Marcia Evanick, veteran Silhouette and Loveswept author, starts off this month with the first in the three-book Wild Rose series, **Wife in Name Only,** in which a marriage undertaken for the sake of the children becomes a surprisingly passionate union. Next up, the talented Jacquie D'Alessandro offers **Kiss the Cook,** the charming tale of a determined caterer—and the sexy financial whiz who tempts her to turn up the heat in her kitchen.

Adam's Kiss, from another promising new author, Patricia Ellis, takes us to a Wisconsin farm, where a dispute between neighbors becomes a kiss across the fence . . . and maybe much more. Tracy Cozzens wraps up the month with her latest book for Zebra, **Seducing Alicia,** the suspenseful story of a scientist who finds herself falling for an unexpected man—without any idea that her new beau may not be exactly what he seems.

Feel the thrill of tenderness and tears, desire and delight. And when you sit back with the four breathtaking Bouquet romances this month, remember to enjoy!

Kate Duffy
Editorial Director

WANTING HIS WIFE

"You want to kiss me when I'm crying?"

"No." Luke shook his head as his thumb stroked her mouth. "I want to kiss you all the time."

"You do?" She arched her body closer to his heat.

"Oh, yeah." Luke's arms slowly went around her and pulled her closer. "What would you do if I kissed you right now?"

She couldn't even contemplate lying to him. She had been waiting for this moment her entire life. Her gaze locked with his and she gave him the truth. "I'll melt."

"Oh, Sue Ellen." Luke took a shuddered breath and arched his hips against hers. "You shouldn't have told me that."

Before she could think of a response, Luke lowered his head and captured her mouth in a kiss. . . .

WILD ROSE:
WIFE IN NAME ONLY

MARCIA EVANICK

ZEBRA BOOKS
Kensington Publishing Corp.
http://www.zebrabooks.com

ZEBRA BOOKS are published by

Kensington Publishing Corp.
850 Third Avenue
New York, NY 10022

Copyright © 2000 by Marcia Evanick

All rights reserved. No part of this book may be reproduced in any form or by any means without the prior written consent of the Publisher, excepting brief quotes used in reviews.

If you purchased this book without a cover you should be aware that this book is stolen property. It was reported as "unsold and destroyed" to the Publisher and neither the Author nor the Publisher has received any payment for this "stripped book."

Zebra and the Z logo Reg. U.S. Pat. & TM Off.

First Printing: May, 2000
10 9 8 7 6 5 4 3 2 1

Printed in the United States of America

PROLOGUE

Sue Ellen Fabian nearly snipped Beatrice's right ear off when Evelyn St. Claire's voice reached over the mirrored partitions dividing The Mane on Main beauty salon. She quickly examined Beatrice's ear and apologized. "I'm sorry, Bea. Are you okay?" There was a tiny red mark but, thankfully, no blood.

Bea held her finger to her lips, demanding silence, and tilted her head in the direction of the voices. There was only one thing Bea liked to do better than spread a fresh piece of gossip, and that was hear a current tidbit of gossip. A lost ear would have been a small price to pay for being the first to spread the latest dirt in Wild Rose, Iowa. Evelyn St. Claire was unknowingly giving Bea an earful.

Sue Ellen usually ignored gossip and any temptation to overhear a juicy tidbit that ran rampant in The Mane on Main. This she couldn't ignore. This concerned her, in a roundabout way.

"I'm telling you, Marilyn, you should have seen little Blake's shirt yesterday. I swear an iron never touched it. And Dalton's sneakers were disgustingly dirty. My poor little grandson had to have been tramping through the cornfields or a cow pasture." Evelyn St Claire's voice rose with horror at the thought of what could have been on the bottom of those tiny sneakers.

Sue Ellen scrunched up her nose and frowned. Blake and Dalton were her godsons, and she didn't see anything criminal in unironed shirts or dirty sneakers. They were boys, just little boys. Boys needed to get dirty once in a while. In her opinion Blake and Dalton needed it more than most other little boys.

"Didn't Luke find another housekeeper yet?" Stella, one of the other hair stylists at the salon, asked.

"No, and it doesn't look like he'll be able to." Evelyn's voice carried clearly over the partition. "Not many women want to be responsible for a widower and two small boys plus be stuck out in the middle of nowhere surrounded by cornfields all day. I don't know how my Tiffany survived out there. I really don't."

It didn't take a psychic to read Evelyn's mind. Her nasal voice carried her opinion of Luke Walker's farm quite well. Sue Ellen could also hear the love Evelyn had for her grandsons, Blake and Dalton.

It had been over a year since Evelyn's only child, and Luke's wife, Tiffany, had been killed in a car accident. The town of Wild Rose was still mourning the beautiful and sweet Tiffany. Herself included. Tiffany had been her best friend in high school. She had been Tiffany's maid of honor at their wedding. She was also given the honor of becoming both Blake's and Dalton's godmother. She missed Tiffany, even

WIFE IN NAME ONLY 7

though over the years their friendship had dwindled down to baby-sitting services when needed. Sue Ellen hadn't minded too much. Since she didn't have a family of her own, she loved spending time with the boys.

"That's a real shame," sighed Stella. "Luke must be working himself into the ground, trying to care for the boys and run the farm at the same time."

"Hmph!" Evelyn gave a small snort. "My grandsons are being neglected, and I won't stand for it. They need a stable home. One with two loving parents, not just some farmer who cares more about corn yields and manure than his own two sons' well-being."

"Luke's an excellent father. I'm sure he's trying real hard to work things out."

Sue Ellen smiled. Stella might have been five years older than Luke, but she had the common sense to appreciate a decent, hardworking and good-looking man. But Evelyn's next words wiped the smile from her mouth.

"He might be trying, but he's not succeeding."

"Well, there's nothing you can do, Ev, but give him as much support as you can. Those boys need their grandparents."

"That's exactly what my lawyer says."

"Lawyer?" Stella's voice squeaked on that one word, and Bea's eyes got so round, Sue Ellen was afraid they might actually fall out of their sockets. Both Bea and herself leaned closer to the partition, not daring to breathe. Neither wanted to miss a word.

"Yes, lawyer. I've decided enough is enough. Blake

and Dalton belong in a two-parent, loving, stable home. Frank and I have decided to apply for custody of the boys."

"But . . . Luke's their father." Stella's voice shook with shock.

"Of course he's their father, and he will be able to visit them any time he wants. It's not like we're moving away or anything. The boys will be raised here in town. They'll be closer to the school and to their friends. It will be for the best, you'll see."

Stella was surprisingly silent while Sue Ellen stared at the scissors in her hand and wondered what Evelyn would look like without either of her ears. Evelyn wanted to take Luke's sons away from him! It was unheard of. It was preposterous. It couldn't be done, could it? Was there a chance Evelyn would succeed and the courts would allow such a thing? Lord, she hoped not. Luke loved his sons.

While she and Luke hadn't been seeing eye to eye in regard to his sons since their mother's death, she could never imagine them living with anyone else. Even their grandparents. Luke was a proud man who never asked for, or expected, any help taking care of his family. The past year and a half had been hard on him and the boys. She had seen them occasionally, but not like in the past.

She was currently trying to get Luke to agree to allow her to throw Dalton a birthday party. Dalton would be turning six in a couple of weeks, and she wanted her godson to have a small party, with just a few of his friends. Luke was being his stubborn self, and she had already been out to the farm twice to confront the mulish man.

This new threat, to both Luke and his sons, she couldn't ignore. Evelyn St. Claire couldn't be allowed to gain custody of the boys, no matter how much money she had to throw around. Luke would never ask for her help, but somehow she would make him accept it.

ONE

The noise was one decibel away from deafening. Sue Ellen grinned as two little six-year-olds streaked past her and headed for the family room, where the rest of the noisy party guests were. If the noise level was any indication, Dalton Walker's birthday party was a complete success. It had been worth every hour she had spent banging her head against a brick wall and arguing with his father. Luke hadn't wanted a party for his son. It wasn't that he had anything against parties, or his son. Luke loved his boys dearly, but he just didn't have the time to plan such an event. It had taken her five trips out to the Walker farm and countless hours to persuade Luke to allow her to throw the party for Dalton. It would be her present to her godson.

She would like to believe she had finally worn the man down, but the sad truth was, Luke was so preoccupied with the threats Evelyn St. Claire was making that he had given in just to shut her up so he could get on to more important matters. She was glad she won the argument, but the victory was a shallow win. Evelyn was in the kitchen this very minute, probably ridiculing the cake. Frank, Dalton's grandfather and Evelyn's husband, was in the family room putting together what had appeared to be a hundred small pieces that would eventually become a spaceship. Evelyn had insisted on coming, and now she insisted on pointing out everything she would have done differently.

Evelyn hadn't been happy to learn that Sue Ellen was handling the party arrangements for her grandson. She felt that she should have been the one throwing the party and had mentioned something about pony rides, a half a dozen clowns and inviting the mayor. Luke had quickly declined her offer and insisted the party Sue Ellen had planned was fine. Evelyn had been in a snit ever since and had shown up at the party with the entire backseat of her Cadillac overflowing with presents for Dalton.

Sue Ellen wasn't impressed.

What did impress her was the way Luke was hanging on to his temper and his sanity. The man was a solid block of control, but she was picking up a couple of signs that cracks were beginning to form. She didn't think she wanted to be around when his control finally snapped. It wouldn't be a pretty sight.

Luke Walker had been under a lot of pressure during the past eighteen months. He had not only lost his young and beautiful wife in an automobile accident, but he was left trying to raise two small boys on his own and run a 350-acre farm. Things had been running more or less smoothly once he hired a live-in housekeeper, Mrs. Johnson. Then, weeks ago, his life once again was thrown into turmoil when Mrs. Johnson left to go live with her daughter in California.

Sue Ellen felt sorry for Luke, but the boys were the ones who really captured her heart. She was determined to bring some much-needed laughter into their lives, and this party was a great start. She only prayed she wouldn't have to fight Luke every step of the way.

She entered the kitchen just in time to hear Evelyn's latest comment. "Firemen! Really, Luke, what were you thinking to order a cake with a fire truck on it?"

"Luke didn't order it, Ev. I did." She forced her mouth to form a polite smile, but she didn't think she was fooling anyone.

"Whatever possessed you to do the party in a fireman motif?" Evelyn waved her hand at the kitchen table that was already set for the birthday boy, his five guests and his older brother, Blake. The adults would just have to fend for themselves.

Motif? Little boys' birthday parties didn't have a motif. A theme maybe, but never a motif. The brightly decorated sheet cake sat in the middle of the table surrounded by a cutout cardboard fire truck that had taken her half an hour to assemble and a half-dozen red and yellow plastic firefighters. Red and yellow streamers were twisted and strung across the ceiling and matching balloons were stuck to the walls by way of static electricity. All in all, Sue Ellen thought she had done a wonderful job, but more importantly, Dalton loved it.

"Dalton told me that he wanted to be a fireman when he grew up." She walked over to the counter and took a sip from the cup of soda she had left sitting there earlier. The ice had melted and now it was lukewarm. White wine, or even a shot of rotgut whiskey, would have been better. The kids at the party she could handle; it was the adults she was having problems with. One in particular.

Evelyn sucked in a breath that depleted the room of half its oxygen. "Luke, you must talk him out of such nonsense immediately."

"Ev, Dalton's only six years old. He changes his mind about what he wants to be when he grows up at least once a month." Luke leaned his six-foot, one-inch frame against the counter and gave Sue Ellen a small tentative smile, as if to say that they were in this together. Sink or swim. "Besides, what's wrong with being a fireman?"

"It's too dangerous! Do you want him to die like my sweet Tiffany did?" Evelyn's voice trembled with grief and tears.

Luke rolled his eyes and muttered, "As far as I know Tiffany never fought a fire in her life." Luke lowered his gaze to the floor as he reached up and started to massage his forehead.

The atmosphere in the kitchen was getting ugly. Sue Ellen needed to change it, before someone said or did something they would regret. Evelyn was on the verge of tears, which was never a good sign, and Luke looked ready to crack. She could tell he had a headache by the way he was rubbing his temple, but it was the small tic beneath his right eye that worried her the most. She never remembered Luke doing that before, and she had known him all her life.

Luke Walker had been her "partner" in their kindergarten class. Whenever the class had gone anywhere they'd had to hold their partner's hand. For an entire school year, Sue Ellen Fabian and Luke Walker were inseparable. It was one of the best years of her life. Then the inevitable happened; she got cooties and he became a pigtail-pulling boy. As they went through school their interests drew them in opposite directions. Luke had joined the football and wrestling teams and become the school's heartthrob and star athlete. She had joined the band, learned to play a mean clarinet and gone to tech school, majoring in cosmetology. In all those years she had never once seen the gorgeous Luke Walker with a twitch.

Now, the twenty-seven-year-old Luke's deep brown eyes were filled with worry and fatigue. His expression was guarded and his complexion was pale under the spring tan he had already acquired from working outdoors every day. A few golden highlights were already marking his light brown hair. Women would, and did, pay a fortune for those same highlights from a bottle, and they never quite matched up to the real thing. Luke appeared to be a man in dire need of diversion, and she was just the woman to give it to him. "I think it's time for the boys to have their cake and ice cream. I'll go get them."

Sue Ellen crossed the kitchen and headed for the family room with as much caution as if someone had planted land mines throughout the house. She was waiting for Evelyn to fling knives into her back. When this party was over and she was once again back in her quiet, peaceful apartment, she was treating herself to a nice long soak in a hot bubbly tub and a chilled glass of wine. If Evelyn opened her mouth about one more thing, she would reward herself with two glasses if she could restrain herself from slapping duct tape across the woman's mouth.

Dalton's shriek of laughter caused her to smile and for now ignore the silent tug-of-war that had been going on in the kitchen. The last thing Dalton or Blake needed was to find out their grandmother was trying to take them away from their father. The boys had been through and lost so much already in their young lives. They loved their father as much as he loved them.

Dalton and his little guests were running around the family room armed with laser guns, an empty water gun that appeared able to hold three gallons of water and a fireplace poker that one little boy was waving like a sword. She snatched the poker as the little heathen ran past. "It's cake time."

She smiled at eight-year-old Blake, who was helping his grandfather snap together the spaceship. He appeared to be in deep concentration as he lined up two pieces and snapped them together. "There's ice cream, too." Blake looked just like his father had when he was that age. Light brown hair and sparkling brown eyes that seemed to take in everything around him. Over the years she had often seen Luke wear that same look of concentration Blake was wearing now.

Dalton, on the other hand, had his mother's nearly

black wavy hair and crystal blue eyes. Dalton was the more talkative and outgoing of the two, but Blake had a quiet strength. Dalton might look more like his mother, but she could see a lot of Luke in the boy.

Loud whoops of laughter accompanied the herd of boys as they barreled down the hall for the kitchen. Blake had joined his young brother in the rush for cake.

Frank St. Claire concentrated on putting the last three pieces of the spaceship together. "You up for the finale, Frank?" In a way Sue Ellen felt sorry for Frank. Being married to someone like Evelyn was enough to invoke anyone's sympathy. Frank had taken Tiffany's death hard, but he didn't appear to be siding with his wife on the issue of where the boys should live. Though he didn't appear to be opposed to the idea either. Frank was sitting on top of the fence, probably praying that he would never have to decide which side he would have to get down on.

Frank put the completed spaceship on the end table. "I shudder to think what those boys will be like after polishing off chocolate cake covered with sugar icing and bowls of ice cream."

"Don't forget the soda." She gave Frank a small smile. "Why do you think I saved the cake part for last? Their parents should be picking up the little monsters in a half hour."

Frank chuckled as he followed her toward the sounds of laughter coming from the kitchen. "There's still Dalton and Blake to deal with."

* * *

Luke watched as the last party guest was driven away by the little boy's mother. He was out of excuses for staying outside. He had to return to the kitchen and not only face Evelyn, but Sue Ellen, too. Evelyn he understood; he knew exactly where she was coming from and what she wanted. It was Sue Ellen who was causing him some concern. The woman was driving him nuts. Or maybe Evelyn had already driven him crazy and Sue Ellen was there to polish him off.

Either way, he wasn't looking forward to returning to the kitchen. Somehow in the past three hours, his once large and spacious kitchen had begun to shrink. It seemed every time he turned around Sue Ellen was right there beside him. She had brushed up against him at least a dozen times. Or maybe he was the one who had brushed up against her. He didn't know anymore. All he knew was that the enticing fragrance she wore was driving him crazy.

Tiffany had worn some heavy musk scent that had set him back a pretty penny every Christmas. Evelyn St. Claire's perfume overpowered the kitchen and half the acreage of his farm. But even with Evelyn's presence in the same room he could pick out Sue Ellen's fragrance. It was a light floral scent that reminded him of Easter mornings.

If Sue Ellen's perfume wasn't enough to contend with, she was wearing a pair of jeans tight enough to affect his blood flow and a soft, fluffy sweater. The dark green of that short-sleeved sweater only drew more of his attention to her golden hair. The long, silky tresses hung to the middle of her back and swayed with her every move. He had caught himself more than once wondering if it was as soft as it looked.

He had been wondering a lot of things about Sue Ellen lately.

"Dad, can we stay out here for a little while?" Dalton rode circles around him on his brand new bike.

Luke pulled his thoughts away from an area to which they had no right going and smiled at the proud tilt of Dalton's chin. This was his first two-wheeler that didn't come with training wheels. Luke was glad now that he had stayed up until nearly one in the morning assembling the thing. Blake was on his bike too, showing off just a tad for his younger brother. "Sure. But I want you both to behave, and don't go near the main road."

"Thanks, Dad," shouted Blake as he skidded to a stop causing his back tire to fishtail.

"Thanks again for the bike, Dad. It's one of my best birthday presents." Dalton flashed him another smile, proudly showing the world where his two front teeth used to be, before chasing off after his older brother.

"What's your other favorite?" he yelled.

"I like them all, but the remote-control fire truck Sue Ellen got me is rad." Dalton waved and headed down the driveway.

He watched them both for a couple more minutes as they raced up and down the long driveway. His heart felt heavy and full of love for his sons. They were too young to be without their mother, but he couldn't change the past. They had to carry on the best they could, and he really was trying his hardest.

Evelyn St. Claire didn't think his best was good enough. And maybe it wasn't, but no one was going to take his sons away from him. They needed him and, just as importantly, he needed them. Evelyn could puff out her grandmotherly chest and hire as many lawyers as she wanted to, but she wasn't taking his sons.

With dragging feet Luke entered the kitchen. The tension that greeted him was almost as thick as Evelyn's perfume. It was obvious she was still being her sweet, charming self. "Well, the guests have all been picked up, and Dalton and Blake are riding their bikes."

"Do they have their helmets on?" Evelyn was sitting at the table, watching Sue Ellen clean up the mess.

"Of course." He went over and held the bakery box open as Sue Ellen slid the remaining cake back inside. Evelyn and Frank had a nice couple who lived in an apartment above their garage and took care of their house and grounds. Only on rare occasions had he ever seen Evelyn do any sort of domestic work.

"It's just as well that the boys are preoccupied outside. I need to discuss something with you, Luke." Evelyn straightened the collar on her suit jacket and gave Sue Ellen a pointed look.

Sue Ellen glanced from the messy table to Evelyn. "I guess I could go straighten up the family room."

"No." Luke took the stack of dirty paper plates from Sue Ellen's hands and tossed them into the waste can. "Sue Ellen can stay to hear whatever you have to say, Ev. Since Tiffany thought enough of her to make her the boys' godmother I'm sure she would have wanted her involved in their lives."

He gave Sue Ellen a reassuring smile, one he didn't feel at all. Evelyn had been hinting all afternoon about some major decision she had made, and to be perfectly honest with himself, he was scared. Evelyn didn't appear to have backed down from her fight to try to get the boys. There had been only one family in Wild Rose that had more money and power than the St. Claires, and that had been the Franklins. Evelyn's maiden name was Franklin, and she was the last of the line. Whatever Evelyn wanted, Evelyn usually got.

Sue Ellen had been Luke's friend his entire life. They had gone through school together. He sensed that Sue Ellen didn't particularly like Evelyn either, though she was polite enough not to say so and had graciously included the St. Claires in the party. He didn't know what Evelyn wanted to talk about, but he might need Sue Ellen in his corner. One thing was for certain: He certainly could use a friend.

Evelyn waved a freshly manicured hand as if to dismiss the entire subject of Sue Ellen. "I've contacted a lawyer in Des Moines who specializes in these types of cases. He assured me that the courts are starting to stray away from parental rights and think more about what's good for the children. Blake and Dalton need a stable home, Luke. One with two loving adults and plenty of opportunities for growth. Frank and I could give the boys that and so much more."

"More's not always better, Ev." Luke watched Frank stare out the picture window to the fields beyond. His father-in-law was being his usual submissive self.

"This isn't personal, Luke."

"Isn't personal!" He stared at Evelyn as if she had just lost her mind. "How can it not be personal? You are talking about taking my sons away from me, and you claim it isn't personal."

"We're not taking them away from you. You would still be their father, and you could see them as much and as often as you want."

"Gee, that's awfully nice of you." His voice dripped with sarcasm, but Evelyn didn't rise to the bait.

"It's quite obvious that you can't take care of them and run this farm at the same time. Look at you; you're exhausted and the house is filthy. There's dust so thick in the living room that I could write my name in it. The other day when I picked up Dalton from kindergarten his shirt hadn't been ironed and there were grass stains on the knees of his pants. You need help with the boys and the house, and since you can't find a housekeeper willing to take on the job, I'm graciously stepping in to help out."

"I found two housekeepers who were willing to take on the job, Ev. It was my decision not to hire either one of them."

Sue Ellen turned and stared at him. "Why?"

"The first one would have put a military drill sergeant to shame, and I honestly think she was in to corporal punishment. The second had shifty eyes and kept staring at the silverware. My gut instinct told me I would have been robbed blind within the first week."

Sue Ellen nodded slowly.

"Is that the kind of housekeeper you want me to hire for your grandsons?"

"Good Lord, no." Evelyn straightened her shoulders and her spine. "It's obvious that you're going through the wrong agency if that's the type of people they are sending you."

He rolled his eyes and wondered again about Evelyn's thinking process. "Now that you know I'm still looking for a housekeeper, we can dispense with this nonsense of the boys living with you. I'm sure eventually they will send one that will meet with my requirements."

"I'm afraid not, Luke. I was hoping we could come to some sort of an agreement without involving lawyers and the courts. It would be so much better for the boys."

"What are you talking about?" He knew there was an edge of panic to his question, but he couldn't help it.

"I just want to warn you in advance that you will be served papers on Monday requesting your appearance in court at the end of the month. You'll be required to prove your ability to raise my grandsons."

"I'm their father! Of course I can raise them." He felt the cold knot of fear clutch his gut. Evelyn was dead serious about this. She was taking him to court, and he would have to prove what kind of father he was.

"From what I've seen and what I told my lawyer, he's confident that we can win the custody battle if it comes to that. You're a farmer, Luke. You don't have a nine-to-five job where you're home at night and on the weekends. Tiffany used to tell me that you put in fourteen- or sixteen-hour days during the busy season. How could you possibly have time for two growing boys, especially with summer approaching and them out of school all day long? What are you planning on doing with them? Putting them to work in the fields?"

Luke reached behind himself and pulled one of the brass and pink upholstered stools away from the counter that separated the kitchen from the dining area. He slowly dropped onto the fancy stool. He couldn't have walked to the table if his life depended on it. His knees had turned to water as fear constricted his heart. "You're serious, aren't you?" He'd never thought Evelyn would push it this far.

"Don't force my hand, Luke. Just give me the boys and we won't have to go to court and air out the family laundry. You know you will always be welcome in our home. You can even spend a night occasionally if you want."

The room was actually going gray around the edges. He wasn't sure if it was the fear or the rage burning inside him that was causing that effect. With the help of a high-priced lawyer, Evelyn was planning on legally stealing his sons. It was impossible. It was preposterous. It couldn't be done, could it? This was America, home of truth and justice. In the majority of cases, truth and justice won out. But as in all things in life, there were exceptions. What were the chances of he and his sons being the exceptions? And did he want to play those odds?

He never saw Sue Ellen move, until she was standing right next to him and she was placing her trembling hand on his shoulder. "Evelyn, the boys aren't going anywhere."

A small smile turned up the corners of his mouth. Sue Ellen's voice held nothing but conviction as she stood up to Evelyn. He almost cheered her on, except that he was wondering why her fingers were digging painfully into his shoulder and why her voice had an undercurrent of trembling behind it. He glanced over and frowned at Sue Ellen's pale face.

"They aren't? Pray tell me why aren't they?" Evelyn's back was so straight, it was amazing that it hadn't snapped in two.

"The boys will have everything you want, Evelyn." Sue Ellen moved a fraction of an inch closer to Luke.

"They will?"

"It was supposed to be secret, until we had time to talk to the boys." Sue Ellen's fingers released his shoulder only to play with the back of his hair where it almost touched the collar of his shirt. "We wanted to wait until the excitement of this party had died down before sitting them down and discussing the future with them."

"What are you talking about?" Evelyn's eyes were frosty cold. Even Frank turned his attention away from the window to stare at Sue Ellen.

Luke had no idea what Sue Ellen was talking about, but he allowed her to continue because Evelyn now appeared as upset as he was. Good. Maybe Sue Ellen had figured out a way out of this mess for him. Whatever it was, it sure seemed to be working. He just wished she would stop playing with his hair like that. It was driving him crazy. So was the fact that her jeans-clad hip was brushing against his thigh and the softness of her sweater was tickling his forearm.

"The boys will have a stable home with two loving adults and Luke will still be able to work the farm and support his family, just as he's always done."

Sue Ellen turned and looked at him. He tried to read her strained expression, but it was impossible. Her lips were trembling and moist, from where she had been nibbling on them. She managed a halfway convincing smile. Her clear blue eyes seem to be begging him for something. What in the world was she up to, and why was she standing so damn close to him that he could hardly think straight?

Sue Ellen turned back toward Evelyn and Frank. "We wanted to give you time to adjust to the idea, but since you are forcing our hand, we're sorry if we hurt you."

Frank spoke for the first time. "What are you getting at, Sue Ellen?"

"Luke and I are getting married."

He heard the words, as if they were coming from a great distance, instead of right next to him. He knew what the words meant, but they didn't make a bit of sense. He was marrying Sue Ellen. Dazed, he watched every drop of color fade from Evelyn's face as her mouth dropped open. Not a sound emerged. Evelyn reminded him of a pasty-face trout. He wondered if she was even breathing.

"You . . . you . . ." Evelyn was stuttering, which

only seemed to increase her temper. "You can't marry Luke!"

"Why not?" Sue Ellen's shoulders went back and her cute little chin lifted an inch or two.

Luke felt like standing up and applauding her. No one had ever stood up to Evelyn before. He wasn't afraid of Evelyn, but he sincerely wanted to make life for himself and his sons more comfortable. To do that, he never tried to antagonize the boys' grandmother.

"That would make you my grandchildren's mother. Tiffany was their mother, not you." Evelyn came to her feet so quickly, the chair she had been sitting on nearly crashed to the floor. Frank's quick reflexes kept it upright.

"I'll be their stepmother, and I wouldn't dream of replacing your daughter." Sue Ellen moved to stand in front of him. It appeared almost a protective gesture. "The boys will have everything you wanted them to have, Evelyn. Surely you can't object to that."

Evelyn looked as if she had just eaten some bad seafood. Her cream-colored silk suit, which she had chosen to wear to a six-year-old's birthday party, had more color than her face. For the first time in her life, Evelyn didn't appear to know what to say. She picked up her purse and headed for the front door. "Come on, Frank. We're leaving."

Frank meekly followed his wife from the room.

Luke saw Sue Ellen move away from him as he played the entire scene through his mind one more time. He wanted to make sure he hadn't missed anything important. One moment he was sick with fear that Evelyn and Frank St. Claire would gain custody of his sons and the next he was supposed to be marrying Sue Ellen Fabian. Impossible. Even his worst nightmares weren't this confusing.

He played the scene over once more. It was just as he thought. Sue Ellen had stood right next to him, running her trembling fingers across the back of his neck, and had blatantly announced that they were getting married. It was the biggest lie of the century.

Sue Ellen nervously bit her lower lip. "Luke?"

He glanced up, pierced her with a look that promised retaliation and roared, "What in the hell did you just do? Are you out of your ever-loving mind?"

TWO

Sue Ellen took another step back and wondered if her eardrums would ever be the same. Luke Walker had rattled the windows when he had shouted. Frank and Evelyn had probably heard him, and they had to be halfway to town by now. She stuck a finger in her left ear and wiggled it. "Geez, Luke, talk about smashing a woman's pride." There wasn't a soul left in the county that didn't now know Luke's opinion on marrying her. She had been wondering when Luke was going to say anything. She had a feeling she had shocked him more than Evelyn when she announced they were getting married.

"We are *not* getting married." Luke folded his arms across his chest and glared at her. "I have absolutely no intention of getting married, to you or anyone else, for that matter."

"I know that." She stuck a finger in her right ear and gave it a wiggle just to let Luke know what she thought of his vocal cords. At least he wasn't singling her out personally from the entire female population. Luke didn't want to marry anyone.

A moment of confusion flashed in Luke's eyes. "You just told the St. Claires that we were."

She rolled her eyes heavenward and prayed for patience. "I lied."

"Why in the world did you do that?" Luke stood up and started to pace. "Now I have to tell Evelyn the truth and then calm her down. She'll be out for blood when she finds out you lied to her. Don't you think I have enough troubles with her already?"

"Luke, sit down and listen for just one moment. I've come up with the perfect plan." At least she hoped it was the perfect plan, or at least a workable one. She'd only come up with the idea as she watched Luke's expression go from annoyance to fear when he learned that Evelyn would be taking him to court. She knew she had to do something to help Luke and the boys, and this was the only plausible idea that came to her. She had kicked her mouth into gear without engaging her brain.

Luke stalked back to the stool and sat down. "What plan are you talking about?"

"Evelyn is taking you to court to get custody of Blake and Dalton. Chances are she won't succeed. You're a great father to those boys; anyone with half a functioning brain cell would see that." Sue Ellen perched herself on the stool next to his and commanded his entire attention as she gathered her thoughts. "I saw the panic and the uncertainty in your eyes, Luke." That look had done some heavy damage to her heart. No father, especially one as great as Luke, should have to go through this kind

WIFE IN NAME ONLY 31

of mental torture. "You're afraid of losing the boys. Admit it."

"Damn right I'm afraid. Wouldn't you be?"

"I'd be terrified and furious, but I'd still be thanking the person sitting next to me who came up with such a brilliant plan." She gave him a wide grin and waited for his appreciation.

Luke didn't say thanks. "Tell me this plan of yours, and then I'll decide if it's brilliant or not."

"What's Evelyn's biggest card?"

"That Blake and Dalton don't have two loving and caring adults to take care of them, and that I need to work the farm to support them."

"No, working the farm is good. It shows steady employment. The courts love steady employment." She gave him a reassuring smile. The man looked like he could use some reassurance—and a very long vacation away from Evelyn and her interfering ways. "It's the working long hours and trying to take care of two small boys and the house at the same time that is her biggest and only card. When Mrs. Johnson was living here taking care of the boys and the house, Evelyn's lawyer wouldn't have taken the case."

Luke nodded in agreement. "Evelyn would have been laughed out of court."

"Correct. So what you need is time to find just the right housekeeper. I've given you that time."

"How, by telling Evelyn and Frank we're going to get married?"

"No, by announcing our engagement. Most engagements last for months, some even for years." She saw the light of understanding beginning to dawn in his deep brown eyes. "Some engagements are even broken, say when a certain farmer finds and employs a suitable housekeeper."

"This is a pretend engagement so Evelyn will get off my back." Luke seem to be thinking her plan through. "There are a lot of bad points to this plan."

"Yeah, the main one being the possibility that Dalton and Blake will find out about it and expect us to really get married." She bit her lower lip and thought for a moment. "Evelyn will be pumping them for everything they know, so let's assume they *will* find out about our so-called engagement. I think if we handle it right and don't make too big a deal about it, it could work out okay."

"Maybe, but what about when the engagement is broken? We'll be the talk of the town. I'm not too worried about what they say about me, since I'm pretty well isolated out here. It's you I'm concerned about."

"Why? Just because I already have one broken engagement doesn't mean I can't have another strikeout." Luke would have to remember Ron, her ex-fiancé. The last thing she wanted was sympathy, so she lightened her voice and pretended the whole thing never mattered. "I heard a woman has to have three strikes before they take her out of the game. I'll be good for one more strike after you."

"Don't you take anything seriously?"

"I'm taking Evelyn's lawyer seriously, Luke. Do you really want to run the risk of losing the boys?"

"No, but why should you do this for us? I know what the boys and I would be getting out of this, but what will you get besides being the talk of the town when the engagement is called off?"

"I get the peace and satisfaction of knowing Evelyn can't take Dalton and Blake away from their father."

"You hate Evelyn that much?"

She smiled sadly and shook her head as she stood up and started to clean off the counter. "No. Evelyn's not too bad once you get to know her. She really does love those boys, but she's going about it all wrong. Instead of fighting you, she should be helping you." Three empty red paper cups with Dalmatians and fire hydrants all over them landed in the trash can. "I'm doing this to protect my godsons. They are the light in my life and I love them both very much. They belong with their father."

"Do you really think we can pull this off without hurting Dalton and Blake? They've already been hurt enough."

"We'll have to be careful and play the whole thing down. Make sure there're no expectations and things like that. The alternative is for them to find out their grandmother wants to take them away from you. Imagine the stress that would put on the boys. They would feel like they would have to choose between their own father, whom they love very much, and their grandmother, whom they also love. They will also be living in fear of the day someone could come and pack them off to go live with Grandmom. Even when the courts side with you, Luke, that fear could be with them for a very long time. So the question now is, which is the lesser evil?"

"It's a hell of a decision, isn't it?"

"At least now you have a choice." Sue Ellen continued to wipe down the counter. A few quick glances at Luke and she knew he didn't like either choice. Who could blame him? Two years ago the man had everything: a gorgeous and loving wife and two beautiful sons. A freak car accident had taken his wife, leaving him in the position of either pretending to be engaged to another woman or risk the possibility of losing his sons. To her the decision was easy, but to Luke an engagement, even a pretend one, had to feel like an assault against the memories of Tiffany.

Tiffany St. Claire Walker had been the reigning crown jewel of the beauties of Wild Rose, Iowa. Tiffany had been the homecoming queen, the prom queen and the captain of the Wild Rose High School cheerleaders. Tiffany could have had any boy in high school, and she went for the cream of the crop, star quarterback Luke Walker. They had made the perfect pair. Months after graduation they had the perfect wedding and went on to produce two perfectly wonderful little boys. Luke's and Tiffany's lives had been blessed until that fateful fall night eighteen months ago.

Why would Luke want to even pretend to be engaged to someone like her? *Cute* had been one of the nicest compliments she had ever received. Tiffany had been gorgeous, vibrant, a social butterfly. She, on the other hand, preferred quiet evenings, a good book and beautiful sunsets.

A fiery blush swept up Sue Ellen's face and she quickly turned her back on Luke before he spotted her embarrassment and read more into it than was there. "Why don't you think about it and let me know later?" She rinsed out the dishcloth and went over to the table, which still had icing smudges and cup rings all over it. "I'll finish cleaning up in here. Go outside and enjoy the boys for a while."

"You don't have to clean up anymore, Sue Ellen. I'll get it later." Luke stood up and stretched the kinks out of his back.

"Nope, a deal's a deal. I said I'd throw the party, and that meant setting it up and taking it all down." She waved the cloth in the direction of the door. "Go enjoy the boys. I bet you don't spend a lot of time with them just relaxing and enjoying life."

"Who has that kind of time?"

"You do right now. You've got an hour, and then I'm out of here."

"Call me selfish, but I'm taking you up on the offer." Luke headed for the door, but before he opened it he turned and seemed to study her face for a moment. "How is it you know that I need to be with my boys right now, right this very minute?"

"It's what any good father would need. There's one thing I do know about you, Luke, and that is that you're a great father to those boys. Never doubt it."

Luke nodded once and then he was gone.

Sue Ellen took a deep breath and slowly released it. Why was it that Luke's presence dominated any room he was in? Now the kitchen felt spacious once again.

Standing in front of Luke and the St. Claires and announcing that she and Luke were getting married was one of the hardest things she had ever had to do. It had revealed one of her secret fantasies—the one she'd had when she was fifteen years old and had thought the sun rose and set with Luke Walker. He had been her and just about every other girl in Wild Rose High's secret crush. The fantasy had died a slow but natural death as soon as Luke and Tiffany became a pair. Nobody could compete with such perfection.

She had squared her shoulders, prayed Luke would understand her reasoning and announced their impending marriage. For Blake and Dalton she would walk around town pretending she was marrying their father. Now the only question that remained was whether Luke was desperate enough to go along with her plan.

Time would tell. Meanwhile she had streamers to take down and balloons to pluck off the walls. Then there was the family room to tackle. Sue Ellen pushed thoughts of Luke and girlhood fantasies out of her mind and started to concentrate on cleaning up.

By ten-thirty that night Sue Ellen was curled up in bed with a good book. The mystery she had started the night before was heating up into a great, thought-provoking puzzle. Only three chapters to go and still she hadn't figured out who the murderer was. There were three likely suspects, any and all of whom had motivation and opportunity. She took a sip of the tea she had just made for herself and started the next chapter. She hadn't even finished the first paragraph when the phone on the nightstand rang. She picked it up before the second ring. "Hello?"

WIFE IN NAME ONLY 37

"Sue Ellen, it's Luke. I hope I didn't call too late."

She ignored the way her heart seemed to pick up an extra beat just at the sound of his deep, rich voice. "No, not at all. I was just settling down with a book. What's up? Blake and Dalton are okay, aren't they?" The way both boys had polished off cake and ice cream at the party, she had been worried that they would both get tummy aches.

"They've been fast asleep for over an hour. I had to talk Dalton out of sleeping with the remote-control fire truck you gave him today." There was a slight hesitation before he said, "I thought the party was going to be your present to him."

"It was, and so was the truck. I saw it the other day and just knew he would love it." She marked her page and placed the book next to her on the bed. "I think all little boys want to be a fireman at one time or another. Didn't you?"

"No. There's only one thing I wanted to be."

"What was that?" She already knew his answer.

There was a smile in his answer. "A farmer."

She grinned. "I kind of figured that one." Luke Walker didn't strike her as the kind of man who would be stuck doing something he didn't want to do for a living. Running a farm would be just a lot of long hours and hard physical work for someone who didn't want to do it.

Luke's voice went from lighthearted to hesitantly serious. "I've been giving this plan of yours some thought. I'm still not sure whether it's brilliant or not, but it could buy me some time."

"Time is what you need so you can find a good

housekeeper." When she had left Luke's house hours earlier, he still hadn't made up his mind if he wanted to go along with her plan or not, and she hadn't pushed him. But there had been a speculative look deep within his eyes. He had been thinking, and thinking hard.

"You do know that if we go through with this plan of yours, the whole town, and especially Evelyn, will think it's strange if we aren't seen in each other's company."

"That could be easily solved, if you just accept some of my help with the boys. I really don't mind pitching in and you know I love spending time with them. Tiffany used to leave them with me all the time. Now I don't get to see them as much as I used to, and I miss that." She took a deep breath and blurted out what had been on her mind for quite some time. "I know it's hard for you to accept the help, Luke. It's not charity, believe me. I really adore your boys, and the only thing I'm expecting in return is an occasional smile from them."

"It doesn't seem like a fair trade. Dalton and Blake can be a handful. Besides, when will you have the time? You work full-time at the Mane, right?"

"Tuesdays and Sundays I have off, plus Wednesday afternoons. I could be out at your place on Tuesdays and Wednesdays in time to meet Dalton's eleven-thirty kindergarten bus. I could spend some time with him, meet Blake's bus at three-thirty and then do something with both boys. It will give you some much-needed time to plow a field or whatever it is farmers do."

WIFE IN NAME ONLY 39

"No one's going to believe we're planning on getting married if all you do is baby-sit my boys."

"Fine. Next Sunday afternoon we can take the boys to see the new Disney movie that just opened and maybe stop for pizza or something. The boys would love it, and it would give you a few hours to relax. People will see us all together and come to their own conclusions." *Plus it would keep my thoughts from drifting where they have absolutely no business straying.* A real date with Luke, without the boys as a buffer, would be too tempting.

"I know it's been a long time since I've been out on a date, Sue Ellen, but I really don't think a Disney movie with two boys in tow counts as one. I think the town and Evelyn will be expecting to see something a little more serious on our part."

"Fine"—she put as much sarcasm into her voice as she could muster—"get yourself a baby-sitter, pack your pajamas and spend next Saturday night on my couch. The town will take us seriously enough then." It was either use sarcasm or issue an invitation that had nothing to do with her couch or pajamas.

"Your reputation will be shot to hell."

She laughed. She couldn't help it. Luke was worried about ruining her reputation. Hell, having Luke Walker spend a night in her apartment, and presumably in her bed, would *boost* her reputation. She'd be the envy of every female from eighteen to ninety. Then again, Esther Gerard was ninety-six, and she'd been known to check out the young widower during Sunday services. Luke obviously didn't know his own appeal to the opposite sex.

"I don't see what in the hell is so funny." Luke sounded a mite confused and upset.

"Sorry. It's just that I'm a little too old to be worried about my reputation." At twenty-seven, and never married, the town of Wild Rose basically considered her a little long in the tooth. Not exactly an old maid, but she was definitely sitting up on the remainder shelf. If you graduated from Wild Rose High and were a female, you basically had two choices—one was to go to college and then move to some big city so your parents could spend all their time bragging to the folks in town about how well you were doing. The other choice was to find some local boy, get married and raise a half dozen little ones.

She never found a local boy she had been willing to spend her life with, never mind falling in love with him. Four years ago she had met Ron Clemant when her car broke down outside of town. Ron was from Penryn, a small town about ten miles out. Ron had been thirty years old to her twenty-three. The seven-year difference hadn't mattered. Six months after she had blown her water pump they were engaged. Three months after they announced the engagement, it had been broken. As far as the town knew, it had been by mutual consent. She had ignored all the whispered speculation and had gotten on with her life. Ron had married someone else nine months after their last good-bye.

She would become the subject of whispered speculation once again if Luke agreed to go along with her plan. At least this time she already knew the ending and would guard her heart.

"Maybe you don't care about your reputation, but I certainly do." Luke was beginning to sound frustrated. "The gossip is going to be bad enough when we break the engagement. I'll be darned if there's going to be additional talk about how my truck was parked outside your place for the entire night."

"Luke, I was joking about you spending Saturday nights on my couch." The man needed to either get a sense of humor or relax some. The old school friend Luke Walker had had a great sense of humor; she wondered where it disappeared to in these past couple of years. It had been missing even before Tiffany's death. She wondered if he'd outgrown it, or had something happened to squash it?

"I believe the town will think it's strange if we aren't seen with the boys in tow. They are part of you, Luke. Marrying you would be a package deal, three for the price of one. So I say it's got to be a family courtship or there will be plenty of talk."

"You might have a point there." There was a lengthy pause and a tired sigh. "So, what you are suggesting is we go all over town as one big happy family."

"No, that would be overkill, Luke. What I'm suggesting is that I spend more time out at your place and occasionally we head into town for ice cream, pizza or a movie. You know, family places." The last thing she wanted was to be looking over some candlelit dinner at Luke, all dressed up and gazing at her adoringly. Hell, she wouldn't be able to control herself and would probably make a complete fool of herself as she climbed over the table and attacked the man.

"How long do you think we could fool everyone?"

"How long do you think it will take for you to find a decent housekeeper?"

"The way it's been going, it might be months."

"No problem." She crossed her fingers and prayed. "Summer will be here before you know it, and everyone will be so busy doing their own thing that they won't have time to keep track of what we're doing."

"True." Luke cleared his throat. "So, Sue Ellen, you really won't mind pretending we're engaged to keep Evelyn off my back?"

"I wouldn't have suggested it if I minded, Luke." Lord, she was going to be engaged to Luke Walker, the most gorgeous man who ever walked the hollowed halls of Wild Rose High. If her friends could see her now. Hell, they were going to see her, and they were going to want every juicy detail. But there weren't going to be any details, juicy or otherwise.

"So, I guess this means we're engaged." Luke's voice cracked on the last word.

The man sounded thrilled to pieces at having her name and his linked together through the town gossip mill. "I'll be out there Tuesday to meet Dalton's bus. We can discuss our strategy then. In the meantime, will you do me one favor, Luke?"

"What's that?"

"Relax. What can go wrong?"

* * *

WIFE IN NAME ONLY 43

Luke stared at the young woman sitting across the kitchen table from him and remembered Sue Ellen's famous words from two weeks ago: *Relax. What can go wrong?* Plenty could and did go wrong with their bogus engagement. One of those things was sitting across from him, stripping him naked with her gaze and blowing bubbles. Huge pink bubbles that matched the streak in her unnatural white-blond hair.

He only had himself to blame for this. He had been so desperate to find a housekeeper this morning that he had agreed to interview a woman who, as the agency had so nicely put it, didn't quite meet all his requirements. So far he hadn't figured out what requirements Miss Jenna Jones did meet. Her résumé said she was twenty-two, but she appeared to be eighteen, and by the look of her two-inch-long red fingernails had never done an hour of housework in her young life.

With a weary sigh, he realized he should have questioned the agency on exactly what requirements this latest applicant didn't meet before agreeing to the interview. The woman had driven a good distance to be interviewed. The least he could do was ask her a couple of questions before sending her on her way. The first two being, where in the hell was her bra and what happened to the rest of her skirt? He stared over her shoulder at the calendar on the wall and wondered when he had gotten so old. He was beginning to feel ancient.

"Can I ask you why you think you would be good

at being a housekeeper and a nanny to my two young sons?"

"Housekeeping is easy. . . ."

"It is?" In the past several months he hadn't noticed one darn thing easy about keeping a house. As Evelyn had pointed out, on more than one occasion he had been doing a lousy job at it.

"Sure. My mom's been doing it her entire life, how hard can it be?"

He tried to hide his grimace, but he didn't think he succeeded. "What about taking care of two active boys?"

"Oh, that will be the easy part. I have five younger brothers."

"You help take care of them?"

"No, that's my mom's job." Miss Jones crossed her legs. "But I know all about boys."

By the way her skirt was riding up her thighs and from that hungry look in her eyes he would bet she did. She probably knew more about what boys liked than he did. He glanced at the clock and desperation clutched at his chest. He was out of time. Miss Jenna Jones had been his last hope. There was no way he would allow this woman to live in his house and raise his sons. "Can you cook, Miss Jones?"

"Sure can." She blew another bubble, sucked it into her mouth and popped it. "I can do fried eggs, bagels, toast and anything that comes with microwave directions. My mom's a fantastic cook, so maybe she could send me some of those instruction things."

"You mean recipes." He wanted to ask if her mother would want the job. The woman sounded perfect. "Did you fill out a questionnaire at the agency concerning your job skills?" He planned to call the agency as soon as he could politely get Miss Jones out of his kitchen.

"Sure did." Miss Jones gave him a saucy wink. "I had to fib a little bit here and there about some of the stuff, but I've been up front with you." Her gaze seemed to travel down his chest and rest on his lap.

"I appreciate that. Honesty is very important during an interview." It also would have helped tremendously on the agency application. If Miss Jones had been a tad more accurate on the application, this interview never would have taken place and his hopes wouldn't have been grounded in the dust the moment he opened the front door and saw her standing there. He stood up, hoping she would take the hint that the interview was over.

"So, do I have the job?" Miss Jones stood and once again amazed him at how well she managed to walk around on top of three-inch platform shoes.

"I'll let the agency know by tomorrow. There's one more applicant coming this afternoon for an interview." What was one more "fib"? He couldn't be cruel and tell her "Not in a million years" to her face. The kid obviously needed a job, just not the one he was offering. "I'd like to thank you for driving all the way out here."

"No prob." Jenna picked up her purse, roughly the size of New Jersey, and swung it over her shoulder. "I'll call the agency first thing in the morning."

Luke held the front door open and watched as she headed out the door with a sassy grin. The late-morning sun reflected off the fake diamond stud in her nose. Blake and Dalton would have loved her. Evelyn would have had a coronary.

Luke slowly closed the door and listened to Miss Jones's mufflerless car head on down the driveway and into the distance. What in the hell was he going to do now?

Evelyn St. Claire had known he had been bluffing about the engagement the whole time, or at least she had suspected. He had just gotten the boys on their school bus that morning when the phone had rung. It had been Evelyn's lawyer. He had been inquiring as to when exactly the wedding was going to take place. Luke had been speechless with shock. Then the lawyer explained that with the upcoming marriage there wasn't any recourse for Mrs. St. Claire to take, unless Sue Ellen had something in her background that would deem her an unfit mother. Luke had been insulted for Sue Ellen and had told the lawyer where to get off before he had slammed down the receiver.

He'd barely started to comprehend the ramifications of that phone call when the agency had called to tell him they'd just taken an an applicant who might meet some of his requirements. He had been so desperate that he'd cut the poor woman at the agency short and told her to send the woman out for an interview immediately.

All morning long he had been praying for June Cleaver, and what he'd gotten was Fran the Nanny, only younger and with a Iowan accent. Sometimes life wasn't fair.

WIFE IN NAME ONLY 47

Sue Ellen's plan, even if it had been filled with holes, had seemed workable. He had privately given it a good two months before folks started bugging them about setting a date. His fingers had been crossed that a housekeeper could be found before the questions started. Luck obviously wasn't on his side.

He glanced around the kitchen. That wasn't entirely true. Luck had been present when Sue Ellen chose to be his pretend bride-to-be. The woman had thrown her heart and soul into helping with the boys and with the house. They had argued that first day when he had come inside to relieve her of watching the boys and to start dinner. He had stepped inside the kitchen only to find it immaculately clean and a pot roast with all the trimmings cooking in the oven. Help with his sons he could accept, but he had drawn the line at having Sue Ellen clean their house. Amazingly enough, he had somehow managed to lose that argument and ended up eating one of the best meals of his life. Then again, as long as he didn't have to cook it, any meal would have been great. The boys must have thought the same thing because they both had asked for seconds.

Anger at the lawyer and his stupid insinuation about Sue Ellen's past burned in his gut. The man was an idiot. Sue Ellen would make a wonderful mother. The question was, why wasn't she one already? He'd never really thought about it before, but he didn't remember the men in Wild Rose being so stupid or blind. Someone should have married her a long time ago.

A deeper burning rage, centered entirely on Evelyn, caused him to sit down and concentrate on taking deep, calming breaths. What had he ever done to that woman to make her hate him so? The entire time he had been married to Tiffany he had tolerated Evelyn's comments and sometimes downright interference. Since Tiffany's death, he had made sure Evelyn and Frank had plenty of time with the boys. His own parents had moved to Scottsdale, Arizona, shortly after he and Tiffany had gotten married. His father's health pretty much kept him in Arizona, so the boys naturally grew closer to Tiffany's parents. Never once had he refused Evelyn or Frank the opportunity to see their grandsons. So why was she fighting so hard to take them away from him?

Because of Tiffany, their only child. Evelyn was heartbroken and trying desperately to hold on to the only things left of her child. Tiffany's sons. He knew why Evelyn was doing this, and even on one level understood her reasoning, but it didn't mean he had to like it or sit back and allow it to continue. Blake and Dalton needed their father, more now than ever before. He refused to fail them as he had their mother.

Luke heard Sue Ellen's car pull into the driveway and wondered how he was going to break the news to her. Sue Ellen had been busting her butt the past two weeks, making sure the plan was working and taking care of his sons and home. She was a real trooper.

A loud knock on the front door was immediately followed by it being pushed open. Sue Ellen practically fell into the kitchen. Luke jumped up and grabbed the two shopping bags she carried. He stared at the overflowing bags in wonder. "You bought food?"

"Blake requested lasagne and you didn't have any of the ingredients." Sue Ellen pushed the door closed and hurried past him, grabbing one of the bags as she went.

"My son asked you to make him lasagne?" This was getting way out of hand. Blake had no right to ask anything of Sue Ellen. He placed the other bag on the counter.

"Oh, he didn't ask." Sue Ellen started to unpack the bags. "The other day he mentioned to me that it had been a long time since he had it and wanted to know if I knew how to make it." Sue Ellen smiled at him as she pulled boxes and jars from the bags. "I told him I did."

He slowly lowered himself onto a stool and watched as Sue Ellen took over his kitchen. There was such a natural grace and ease to her movements. She looked like she belonged in his kitchen. A glimmer of an idea began to form in the back of his mind.

"I thought I would have Dalton help me make it."

"What? The lasagne?" Dalton and spaghetti sauce didn't sound like a good combination to him, but leave it to Sue Ellen to want to include his son on the preparations. Sue Ellen was a natural-born mother. The spark of the idea blazed brighter.

"Sure. Dalton loves to cook." Sue Ellen turned to the refrigerator and put away the fresh vegetables she had picked up for a salad. "The other day he helped me peel the carrots."

The idea turned into a revelation. Why in hell hadn't he thought of it before? It would solve all his problems, permanently. "You really love the boys, don't you?"

"Of course I do. What kind of silly question is that?" Sue Ellen shook her head as she placed boxes and jars into his cabinets. She looked like she had been unpacking groceries in this kitchen for years.

"You would make a wonderful mother, Sue Ellen." He thought he saw her hand tremble as she shoved another box deep into the cabinet, but he might have been mistaken. "Why don't you have any kids of your own by now?" At twenty-seven she was still young enough to start a family; heck, she had plenty of child-bearing years left. The way she took care of his sons told him that she really loved children. It seemed strange that she didn't have two or three of her own playing at her feet.

Sue Ellen kept her back to him as she straightened a shelf crammed with half-empty cereal boxes. "Call me old-fashioned, but I believe one should have a husband before one has babies."

"You don't have a boyfriend or anyone special in your life right now, do you?" He didn't think she did, but he needed to be sure.

Sue Ellen turned around and frowned. "What's with the questions, Luke?"

"I'm making sure there's no one waiting in the wings for you when this engagement ends." It still seemed strange to him that she was free and single.

WIFE IN NAME ONLY 51

"Do you honestly believe that a boyfriend or someone special in my life would sit back and wait while I pretended to be engaged to someone else?"

"Not if he had a lick of common sense he wouldn't." He tilted his head and studied the pretty picture she made standing in his kitchen as if she owned it. "You're not in love with anyone, are you?" How did she manage to fill out a pair of jeans with such perfection? The baggy sweatshirt, which appeared to have been left over from her high school days, looked soft and cuddly.

Small, delicate hands landed on her hips and her frown turned into a glare. "What are you trying to get at, Luke? Just come right out and say whatever's on your mind. Something has been eating at you since I walked in."

"I have a proposal for you."

"Shoot." Sue Ellen tilted her head, and the glare turned to curiosity.

"What do you think about us getting married for real?" He blanched when he saw all the color drain from her face and her mouth sag open. Not his smoothest proposal, but then, he had only asked one other woman to become his wife. "You already love the boys, and they really do need a mother. You would be my wife, in name only."

THREE

Wife, in name only? What in the world did that mean? There was only one way to find out. "What do you mean by name only?" Luke Walker wanted to marry her. Really marry her? It made no sense at all.

"You would legally be my wife, but we wouldn't be living together as man and wife."

Luke wasn't making one bit of sense. "We'd get married and I'd still be living at my apartment?"

"No"—Luke appeared to be blushing—"you'd be living here. We just won't be sharing a bed. You can stay in the spare bedroom."

"Ah, now I get it. We won't be sleeping together." Now she was the one blushing. Luke wanted a permanent mother for his children, but he wasn't willing to sleep with her to get it. If her ego took another hit like that one, they would have to put it on life support. "What happened to our plan?"

"Evelyn called our bluff. Her lawyer called me this morning wanting to know the exact wedding date."

"Ouch." So that was what prompted his unexpected proposal.

WIFE IN NAME ONLY 53

"Then the employment agency called, and they sent out another applicant for the housekeeper position."

"I'm gathering that didn't turn out so well either." That was the third applicant since their pretend engagement had been announced two weeks earlier. Luke was scraping the bottom of the domestic help barrel. "What was wrong with this one?"

"Besides being about eighteen, having white and pink hair and her nose pierced?"

"There was more?" She bit the inside of her cheek to keep from chuckling.

"Her housekeeping experience comes from watching her mother do it. She couldn't cook and had absolutely no experience with children." Luke shuddered. "Blake would be tattooed by June and Dalton would be the only kid in his Sunday school class with a pierced eyebrow."

Sue Ellen couldn't help it; she burst out laughing. "I would have hired her just to see Evelyn's face when they met for the first time."

Luke shuddered. "It was tempting, but I figured it wouldn't help my cause if this does end up in court."

"That's true. It would just be one more thing Evelyn could use against you." She folded the two empty paper bags and put them away. During the last two weeks the fatigue and strain had slowly faded from Luke's face. This morning every ounce of it was back, and then some. She wanted to drive into town and confront Evelyn about her interfering ways. If Evelyn spent her time and effort helping Luke instead of fighting him, there wouldn't be any cause for concern.

Luke would have plenty of time for his sons and to work the farm. "It's a sad state of affairs when a man's profession can be used against him in a court of law."

"It's not the profession, it's the hours I have to put in." Luke paced to the other side of the room. "I'll sell the farm, move into town and get a job where I'll be home every night before I allow Evelyn to take my sons."

"You'd sell the farm?" Luke Walker *was* this farm. This was his dream. This was his life. He would give it all up for his sons. Was there any wonder her heart cried for this man?

"As a last resort, yes." Luke stared out the large picture window at the newly turned fields beyond.

"Well, at least I'm not the last resort." She studied his proud profile and lean body.

Luke turned toward her. "What's that mean?"

"It means you would marry a woman you don't love before you would sell this farm." She tried to give him a small smile to soften her words, but her heart just wasn't in it. She really shouldn't allow his words to hurt so much.

"It means I would marry a woman who would make a wonderful mother for my sons before I would sell their heritage." Luke leaned against the windowsill, crossed his arms across his chest and frowned. "Blake and Dalton need a mother, just as much as they need a father and financial security."

Sue Ellen bit her lower lip and stared at the man who was offering her the world, or at least a good portion of it. Luke was offering her something more precious than gold. He was giving her her dream,

WIFE IN NAME ONLY

and on a silver platter, no less. Luke would be giving her the one thing she couldn't have on her own, or even with the help of a willing partner. Luke was blessing her with children. Blake and Dalton would be the children she could never have. Together they would become a family.

Her engagement four years earlier to Ron Clemant had ended when she had gone to her gynecologist for birth control and had been given some devastating news. Her uterus was slightly tilted, and the chances of her becoming pregnant weren't very good. She would probably never carry a child within her body. Ron, who had also wanted a large family, had put on a brave face, but the engagement had been broken within two weeks. Ron had never come right out and said it was her inability to have children that had changed his mind, but she had known the truth. No man wanted half a woman. Her inability to have children made her feel like she wasn't a whole woman. As far as the town knew, the engagement had been broken mutually and there had been no hurt feelings.

Her feelings had not only been hurt, they had been crushed. More by her barrenness and the death of her dreams of a family of her own though, than by Ron. It had taken her a while, but she realized she hadn't been in love with Ron; she had been in love with the idea of being in love and starting a family. She had silently buried the dream and had gotten on with her life. Now, Luke was offering to give her back that dream.

Since he had been very specific about not sharing

a bed, the topic of her being barren wouldn't be an issue. Luke didn't want any more children; he just wanted to keep the ones he already had. Luke wouldn't care if he was marrying only half a woman. Her dream was within her grasp; all she had to do was say yes.

She glanced at the clock and realized that Dalton's bus would be there any moment. She quickly headed for the door. "I have to go meet Dalton's bus."

Luke's hands gripped the back of a chair. "Would you at least think about my proposal?"

"I already have." There really hadn't been anything to think about. She had known her answer the moment he had asked the question. She opened the door and felt the warmth of the sun bathe her face. Spring, with her cool breezes and sweet scents, had finally arrived.

"And . . . ?"

She squinted up at the sun because she didn't want Luke to see her tears. He wouldn't understand them any more than she did. She would be getting her dream of a family. It didn't matter that her husband wouldn't love her or share her bed. Luke was an honest, hardworking man who loved his sons. Any woman would be proud to call him her husband. "Yes, I'll marry you."

Without waiting for Luke's reply, she closed the door behind her and headed down the long driveway to where it met the main road. She could see the yellow bus in the distance and hurried her pace as she wiped at the tears. Luke Walker was giving her his sons to raise. What did she need with his heart?

***

Luke nervously paced the small area near the back door of the church. Sue Ellen wasn't late for their wedding, but she wasn't early, either.

His memory slipped back nine years to the bright September day when he and Tiffany had gotten married in this same church. Tiffany had been barricaded in the choir room for over an hour before the ceremony had even started. She had been surrounded by her mother, her grandmother, Sue Ellen, six bridesmaids, two flower girls and a hair dresser. Their wedding and reception had been a three-ring circus, with Evelyn acting as the ring master. Wild Rose had never seen such a wedding before or since; Tiffany St. Claire had shocked her parents and the entire town by marrying a local farm boy who had nothing but a strong back and love in his eyes. The strong back had kept a roof over their heads, food in their bellies and a few luxuries. But the love hadn't been enough. Tiffany had needed so much more from him. She had needed things he didn't understand. He had given her everything he had, and it still hadn't been enough.

He had failed Tiffany. The ultimate failure had been the night she had died. She never should have been behind the wheel of that car, and he had only himself to blame. Tiffany's death still weighed heavily on his soul and his conscience.

This marriage to Sue Ellen was going to be different. This was purely an arrangement for the benefit of his sons. There was no love to murk the marital waters.

Sue Ellen was a strong, independent woman who wouldn't be depending on him for anything besides financial support. The farm was holding its own in bad times and prospering in good ones. He wouldn't fail Sue Ellen. The boys would be getting a mother, and all threats of a long, drawn-out custody battle would be put to rest with two simple words: "I do."

This marriage was the perfect solution to all his problems. There was only one question remaining— one that hadn't been answered to his satisfaction yet, and the reason he was waiting for his bride outside the church instead of inside.

Luke glanced down at Blake and Dalton, who were sitting on the back steps looking handsome with their hair slicked down and in their Sunday best. They were his life, his heart and his very soul. They were his reason for getting up every morning and falling exhausted into bed every night. He would give them anything and everything.

Both boys had been thrilled when he had explained about Sue Ellen and how she was going to become their "stepmom." Blake and Dalton loved their unofficial Aunt Sue Ellen and were anxious for the ceremony and their new life to begin. The past two weeks had been a blur of activity for the boys. They had had questions, but thankfully most of them had been aimed at Sue Ellen, not him.

Sue Ellen handled the boys and their constant questions better than he did. She was going to make a wonderful stepmom.

"Where's Sue Ellen, Dad?" Dalton stood up and started to pace along with him.

WIFE IN NAME ONLY

"Yeah, Dad. Shouldn't she be here by now?" Blake stood up and brushed at the seat of his brown dress pants.

Luke glanced at his watch. Five minutes to the ceremony and still no bride. He wondered if she was getting cold feet. For that matter, he wondered why she had agreed at all. He knew why he had asked her to marry him. The reason had two names, Blake and Dalton. But why had she said yes? What was Sue Ellen getting out of this marriage? He was saved from reassuring his boys that Sue Ellen would be there any minute when a car pulled into the parking lot. He silently sighed in relief. For a moment he had begun to worry.

"She's here!" Blake shot across the parking lot, with Dalton quickly on his heels.

He watched as Sue Ellen's parents and her younger sister, Carrie, got out of the car. Carrie had flown in from California yesterday just to see her sister get married. His gaze went immediately to the rear door as his bride stepped out of the car and greeted his sons with a warm, wide smile. His breath locked in his throat. Sue Ellen looked beautiful when she smiled.

He stood there and watched as Sue Ellen handed her sister the bouquet of flowers she had been holding and reached for his sons' hands. He anxiously waited at the back door as the wedding party and guests made their way across the parking lot. He hadn't wanted a big fancy wedding, and Sue Ellen had agreed with him. He had been expecting her to want the works from half a dozen bridesmaids to a reception with flowing fountains of champagne. Sue Ellen's only request was that her parents and sister be present and that the ceremony be performed in a church. He would have waited the extra weeks the planning of a big wedding would have caused and would have silently suffered through another big production number if Sue Ellen had wished it. What he was getting out of this marriage was far more important than stuffy tuxes and engraved invitations.

He studied his bride and noticed that her smile had slipped from warm and welcoming to a polite and nervous upward curve when she saw him standing there. Even the tight little smile couldn't diminish her beauty today. If anyone had asked him to describe Sue Ellen before this day, he would have said cute, or even perky, in a country sort of way. Now he would have to answer beautiful or even coolly sophisticated. He didn't know if he liked this new perspective of her. One thing was for sure, he wasn't comfortable with it.

Sue Ellen was wearing a knee-length dress that was the exact color of freshly churned butter. A matching short-sleeved jacket covered her shoulders, and a pair of high heels gave her five-foot, six-inch frame some height. Her long blond hair, which was usually loose or pulled back into a ponytail, was swept up into some complicated braid, and delicate pearl earrings graced her lobes.

Not for the first time Luke had to wonder if he was doing the right thing. Sue Ellen certainly didn't look like anyone's mother dressed like that.

"Hi." Sue Ellen stopped directly in front of him "Are we late, or are you early?"

"We were early." Luke nodded toward his sons who were both still holding Sue Ellen's hands. "They were anxious." That was only partly true; they had been eager, but he had been the one to rush them all out of the house.

Sue Ellen smiled down at the boys.

"Hey, Luke, you aren't supposed to see the bride before the ceremony." Carrie Fabian elbowed him in the side and gave him a saucy wink. "Bad luck, you know." Carrie was three years younger than Sue Ellen and lived in Los Angeles. She had been a couple of years behind him in school, but he still knew her. In a town the size of Wild Rose, everyone knew everyone else.

"Bad luck?" Dalton's eyes opened wide and there was a slight tremor in his voice.

Before he could reassure his son, Sue Ellen squatted down, until she was at eye level with the boy. "Carrie's just teasing, Dalton. Your father sees me all the time and there hasn't been any bad luck." Sue Ellen glared at her sister. "Right, Carrie?"

"Right as rain." Carrie ruffled Dalton's black hair.

"Rain isn't right, it's wet." Dalton grinned.

Carrie laughed. "Smart boy you got there, Luke." Her hand reached out and messed up Blake's neatly combed hair. "Do either of you boys know what happens once my sister here goes inside this church and says 'I do' to your old man?"

"We get a stepmom." Blake looked pleased that he answered the question first. He tried unsuccessfully to straighten his hair.

"Well, that's true, but it's something better than that." Carrie was grinning proudly.

"Better than a stepmom?" Dalton looked at Luke with wide, trusting eyes filled with excitement.

Luke didn't know what Carrie was up to, but she had better not disappoint his sons. "Don't look at me, Dalt, I don't know what she's talking about." Sue Ellen's smile told him that she knew and absolutely approved of her sister's teasing.

"What is it, Carrie?" Blake was glancing from adult to adult, looking for clues.

"Do you know what else you both get besides a stepmom?"

"New grandparents!" Dalton jumped to answer. He and Sue Ellen had already sat the boys down and explained how they would be getting a third set of grandparents. Both boys seemed excited by the prospect.

"You already have grandparents." Carrie winked at her parents. "This is better."

"What, what?" Dalton was tired of guessing. He wanted to know the answer

"You're getting an aunt." Carrie threw out her arms in triumph. "Me." She hugged both of the boys. "I'm going to be your Aunt Carrie."

Both of Luke's sons hugged her back and seemed thrilled with the idea of getting a real aunt. Carrie looked just as thrilled to be an aunt.

"Do you know what's the neatest part of having an aunt who lives in California and who only has a chance once or twice a year to come see you?" Both boys shook their heads. "I buy really neat presents. In fact, I seem to have brought two with me this time." She winked at the boys. "I wanted to make a nice first impression. This aunt stuff is all new to me."

WIFE IN NAME ONLY

"Where are the presents?" Dalton was glancing around the church parking lot as if they would suddenly appear.

"Back at your new grandparents' house. I'll give them to you there." Carrie handed Sue Ellen her bouquet and took a boy's hand in each of hers. "I'm going to be a great aunt, you just wait and see."

Sue Ellen's mother opened the door to the church. "I think we'd better head on in. I'm sure the reverend is waiting for us."

Luke gave Sue Ellen's parents a forced smile. He hadn't realized until Sue Ellen mentioned that she wanted her parents at the ceremony that he would be getting another set of in-laws. Evelyn and Frank St. Claire weren't technically his in-laws any longer, but he couldn't close them out of his life. They were his sons' grandparents. His sons were now getting a third set of grandparents and he was acquiring a new set of parents-in-law and a sister-in-law. It was a sobering thought, even though he had always liked Sue Ellen's parents and younger sister. "Could you go on ahead without us? I need to talk to Sue Ellen for a moment."

Mrs. Fabian glanced at Sue Ellen for a moment before nodding her head. "We'll tell the reverend that you'll be right in." She and her husband disappeared through the gray metal door.

"Come on, boys," said Carrie as she ushered them both up the steps. "We'll leave the lovebirds alone."

Luke sighed as the heavy metal door cut off his sons' laughter. Having their father and Sue Ellen referred to as lovebirds had tickled their funny bones.

He faced his bride. "Your mother doesn't seem to like me."

"Right now she's thinking you're about to call off the wedding."

"Why would she think that?"

"She's been suspicious of this whole engagement, wedding thing from the beginning. She said it happened too fast."

"She's right." There wasn't anything else he could say; Sue Ellen's mom was right, everything *was* happening too fast. It had only been two weeks since the lawyer called and wanted the wedding date. Since there was no reason to wait, they had agreed to tie the knot as soon as possible.

"Are you getting cold feet, Luke?" Sue Ellen tilted her head and studied his face.

"No." He jammed his hands into his pants pockets and rocked back on his heels. "That's not the reason I wanted to talk to you."

"What is it, then?"

"I'm curious about one thing." He noticed the paleness of her face under expertly applied makeup and the slight trembling in her hands. Sue Ellen wasn't as cool as she'd first appeared.

"What?"

"Why are you marrying me? We both know why I'm marrying you, but I'm still not clear on your reasons for saying yes to my proposal." That unanswered question had been bothering him for the last two weeks. He wanted an answer before the reverend pronounced them man and wife.

"The boys need a mother and they need to stay

with their father. This is the simplest and easiest way to achieve that."

"We're talking about a life-long commitment here, Sue Ellen. I won't be putting the boys through a divorce, even if you are only their stepmother."

"I'm aware of that, Luke. The boys have been through enough already in their young lives. They don't need any more upset." Sue Ellen glanced at the church in front of them. "I took an oath before God on the day I became Blake's and then again when I became Dalton's godmother. I swore I would always be there for them and to help raise and guide them should something happen to Tiffany or you."

"I don't think the church had marrying their father in mind when you took that vow." He shook his head in disbelief. Sue Ellen was marrying him because she was the boys' godmother?

"I assure you, Luke, this is what I want." Sue Ellen gave him a small smile that never reached her eyes. "I will be a very good mother to your sons."

"I have no doubts about that." He saw the hint of sadness and pain in her clear blue eyes and remembered that she had been engaged before, to Ron Clemant. Ron was now married with one child and another on the way. In all likelihood, his bride was still in love with another man. What a fine pair they were going to be. "Are you sure about this, Sue Ellen?"

"There's not a doubt in my mind." Sue Ellen studied his face once again. "Are you sure you're not getting cold feet?" This time there was a smile in her voice, if not on her face.

"My feet are fine. It's my sanity I'm worried about." He took a hold of her elbow and escorted her up the three stairs to the back door. "Let's get this over with before your mother comes back out here demanding to know what's taking so long."

Nine hours later Sue Ellen closed the book she had been trying to read and leaned farther back into the pillows propped up behind her. She was now a married woman. She was Mrs. Luke Walker and she was spending her wedding night alone in the spare bedroom, with only the current best-selling mystery for company.

She didn't feel married. No woman spending the night with only John Grisham for company would feel married, unless she happened to be Mrs. John Grisham. She had to wonder what exactly made a woman feel married. Just sleeping with a man wouldn't do it. Too many woman slept with too many men for the physical act of making love to be equated with being married. Was it love? Did the married feeling come from being in love with your husband, and having him be in love with you? That wasn't right either. Too many couples that weren't married were in love with each other, and too many married couples weren't in love.

It didn't really matter what made a person feel married. She was married, and eventually she would get used to it. She gave a heavy sigh and glanced around her new bedroom. The antique oak bedroom set had to have been Luke's parents', and she had fallen in love with it immediately. Thankfully, the spare bedroom was her favorite room in the house. She might have been Tiffany's friend in high school, but they surely hadn't shared the same taste in decorating. This appeared to be the only room in the house that Tiffany had never gotten her hands on. Pale green walls and crisp white trim accented the furniture beautifully. White lace curtains let in the sun and a multicolored braided rug cushioned one's feet. A hand-stitched quilt covered the bed and brightened the room with its colors of spring. She had loved the room on sight and was more than willing to fill its closet and drawers with her belongings.

The rest of Luke's house was a nightmare. Oh, Lord, Luke's and her house was a nightmare! A stuffy, pink, frilly nightmare that had only showcased Tiffany's personality. Luke's and the boys' identities were nonexistent, and there was absolutely no room for her to insert her own individuality. She would either be stuck living with Tiffany's taste or she would have the delicate job of eliminating Luke's first wife's personality from what was now her home.

Luke had told her that the house was now her domain and she could do with it what she wanted. She didn't think he had redecorating the entire house in mind. She would have to take it slowly and start with the easiest rooms first. The family room and kitchen were the most used rooms, so that was where she would start. Most of her furniture, back at the apartment, had been castoffs or yard-sale finds. She'd already sold the couch and kitchen set. Gloria, the hairdresser hired to replace her at The Mane on

Main, was interested in not only her apartment but her bedroom set as well. There were only a few items, most of which had been her grandmother's, that Sue Ellen wanted to bring here. One trip into town with Luke's pickup truck would see the job done. The question was, where was she going to put the few chosen pieces? She would worry about that once she got them to the farm. She had more important things to worry about besides an antique secretary, a few decorative tables and a rocker.

She had a husband on the other side of the bedroom wall who, after putting his sons to bed for the night, couldn't seem to get away from her fast enough. She also had two little boys who seemed thrilled with the idea of her becoming their stepmom, but weren't quite comfortable with calling her mom yet. That was okay with her. She understood the confusion they must be going through and wasn't about to push the issue.

It was Luke's behavior tonight that caused her the most worry. She hadn't expected the typical wedding night with Luke. He had been very up-front with his announcement that they wouldn't be sharing the same bedroom, let alone the same bed. But she also hadn't been expecting to be abandoned to her own devices by ten o'clock either. She had envisioned a quiet, relaxing evening talking about the farm, the boys and the future. Instead she had gotten a stiff-looking Luke inquiring if she had everything she needed, then telling her it was late and he'd see her in the morning.

She had known she wasn't going to be her hus-

WIFE IN NAME ONLY 69

band's lover, but she had been hoping to be his friend. How in the world were they ever going to make a go of this marriage if they weren't even friends? It was a depressing thought.

With a weary sigh, Sue Ellen glanced at the clock and saw that it was now past midnight. She wondered what time the boys got up and what they would want for breakfast. Then there was Luke. Farmers got up early, and she wondered if she was expected to rise at the crack of dawn every day. It was a sobering question, and one she should have asked before taking her vows. Dawn was definitely a four-letter word in her vocabulary. She placed the book on the nightstand, turned out the light and slid farther down beneath the sheets.

There was no doubt about it, marriage would take some getting used to. She wasn't going to solve the problems of the world in one night. She would take every day as it came and count her blessings along the way. She now had a family of her own, and getting up with the roosters was a small price to pay.

As the darkness settled around her and sleep pulled at her tired mind, she had one last vision of her wedding day to carry with her into the dream world and to file away into her memories.

Luke and she had been standing in front of the altar with the reverend when he announced to Luke that he could kiss the bride. Blake and Dalton had giggled and her sister Carrie had heaved a romantic sigh. She had held her breath and waited to see what Luke would do. In all the years she had known Luke, he had never kissed her romantically. She remembered a couple of hugs between them over the years on special occasions—hugs that she always initiated.

Now they were going to share their first kiss as husband and wife and in front of her parents, his sons and God. Her gaze had dropped to his mouth and she had actually felt her knees go weak as desire slammed into her stomach. She had wanted Luke to kiss her, really kiss her as a man would kiss a woman. When she had realized where her thoughts were heading her gaze had shot up to his and she had caught something flash deep and dark within his brown eyes as they stared at her mouth.

Her instinct told her it had been desire, but he had masked it so quickly, she had convinced herself she had been mistaken. Luke didn't desire her. If he did, why would he have put no-sleeping-together as a condition of their marriage? She had been mistaken and his chaste kiss at the altar had proved it. One instant his cool lips touched hers and the next they were gone, and he was turning back toward the preacher.

Embarrassed by her own pounding heart and disappointment, she had glanced at the small group standing at the front of the church. Her mother had looked worried, Carrie had looked confused, but it had been the boys' reaction that had lightened the moment and given her the strength to face Luke once again. Blake and Dalton had both scrunched up their faces and shouted, "Yuk!" She couldn't have agreed with them more.

FOUR

Sue Ellen slowly ran her hand over the pink satin comforter and smoothed out the last of the wrinkles. Her husband of three days slept in a queen-sized bed with plain white cotton sheets and a comforter that would have looked at home in a movie starlet's mansion. The comforter fit the master bedroom's decor. The plain, off-the-shelf-of-Wright's-Department-Store-in-town sheets did not. Luke had bought different sheets since Tiffany's death but had left the rest of the room the same. Why? No man could be comfortable sleeping in a room decorated for a princess.

She glanced around the room and shuddered. Tiffany's idea of decorating a bedroom to be shared with her husband, a man who was most comfortable tilling the soil and watching weather reports, was a massive dose of pink flowers, ruffles, bows and lace. What in the world had Tiffany been thinking? Pink rosebud wallpaper covered the walls. The beautiful double windows that overlooked acres of fields were obscured by layers of frilly white lace that appeared to be billowing in spite of the fact that the windows weren't even open. Tiffany had relegated the beautiful oak bedroom set to the spare bedroom and installed ornate white with gold trim furniture here. Plush, snowy white carpeting covered what was probably oak plank flooring.

What should have been a cozy niche in front of the windows was now the display area for two delicate French design chairs with light pink satin upholstery. Neither chair looked like it would have supported Tiffany's weight, let alone Luke's. A matching satin tablecloth flounced its way around the small, delicate table that was positioned between the chairs. An assortment of family photos, all in gold frames, crowded the tabletop.

She walked across the room and studied the pictures. A smiling Tiffany holding Blake when he was about a month old. Luke and Tiffany at their wedding. Tiffany wearing her homecoming queen's crown as her court was blurred into the background. A sixteen-year-old bikini-clad Tiffany lounging across the hood of what had been a brand-new Ford Mustang she had received from her parents as a birthday present. Tiffany posing royally with a grinning three-month-old Dalton in her arms.

In every one of those photos Tiffany had looked gorgeous and perfect. Every strand of her silken black hair had been artfully combed into place. Lips had been glossed an enchanting red. Even at sixteen, Tiffany had been gorgeous. No braces had ruined her smile, no pimples had ever dared to mark her fair complexion. Hell, Tiffany hadn't even been flat-chested.

How was she ever going to compete with such perfection?

Sue Ellen stopped and stared at the pictures in confusion. Since when did she want to compete with the flawless ghost of Tiffany St. Claire Walker?

"Something wrong, Sue Ellen?" Luke walked into the bedroom and stared down at the assorted pictures. A small frown pulled at his mouth.

She jerked around in surprise. She hadn't heard him come up the stairs. She glanced at his feet and noticed the white socks. Luke had taken off his shoes at the back door. One thing she could say about Tiffany, she had trained the males of this household well. None of them would step a foot into the house with dirty shoes on. "No, nothing's wrong. Why?"

"You looked . . . I don't know, confused, when I came in." Luke glanced away from the photos. "I told you that you don't have to straighten up in here. I can handle one room. You have enough to do with the boys and the rest of the house."

"I was washing sheets this morning and it was no problem adding yours." She glanced around the room, shook her head and smiled. "There was nothing to straighten up in here. I thought husbands were supposed to be messy creatures who left sweat socks and underwear laying all over the place." Luke hadn't moved or touched one thing in the bedroom, beside the blanket on his bed, for three days.

Luke raised one eyebrow. "Someone been giving you advice on husbands?"

"Every woman in town has offered me a tidbit or two since we announced our engagement." She had been receiving more than a tidbit or two since the town discovered that she and Luke had tied the knot in a very small and informal ceremony. She had made the mistake of going food shopping yesterday morning and had run into just about everyone she knew since the time she was born.

Unsolicited advice ran second only to the wild speculation as to why the wedding had been a hurried affair. The consensus in town was that she was pregnant with Luke's child. No one had come right out and asked her, so she couldn't very well stand in the middle of Main Street and deny the rumor. She figured the town would realize she wasn't pregnant in a couple of months when she still wasn't showing.

"Anything I should know about?" Luke seemed amused by the notion.

"It was nothing more than what every mother has told her daughters over the years. Tales of raised toilet seats, wet towels on the bathroom floor, football season and beer can rings on the end tables." She didn't think Luke would want to hear about how eighty-two-year-old Edna Felts had cornered her by the frozen vegetables and given her some womanly advice. Edna had told her to take what she could get and always ask for more, because one never knew what the future held. By the gleam in the old woman's eyes, Sue Ellen knew she hadn't been talking about food or money. Edna had gone through four husbands and was currently courting Harvey Parker. Harvey was seventy-six years old and retired from farming. He played checkers all day long with anyone willing to sit through his daily rendition of how he and his platoon had taken the beach at Normandy on D-Day. Lately Harvey had been seen walking around town with a silly grin splattered across his face, and there was a definite lively spring in Edna's step.

Sue Ellen glanced over at Luke as he picked up his wallet, which had been sitting on top of the bureau. He slid it into the back pocket of his worn jeans, and she had to bite her lower lip to keep a sigh from escaping. Her husband knew how to fill out a pair of jeans. Maybe she should invite Edna over for tea one afternoon and hope for pointers.

"I've got to run into town for a part. Do you need me to pick up anything?" Luke started for the bedroom door.

"No, but thanks for asking." She followed him out into the hallway. One thing she could say about her husband, he was polite and thoughtful. He was always asking her if she needed anything from this place or that. One day he might even ask her if she wanted to come along just for the ride.

Sue Ellen studied Luke's tan jaw and noticed that some of the stubble working its way back to the surface held a golden sheen instead of the darker shade that covered most of the bottom part of his face come evening. That intriguing stubble had been fascinating her for the past three nights. Would it be as rough as it appeared, or was there a softer quality? Her fingers itched to find out.

She closed her hands into fists and purposely looked away from Luke. The narrow hallway seemed to shrink with his presence filling it with his hard body and the enticing scent of soap, open fields and maleness. She pulled her thoughts away from her husband and concentrated on the real reason he had married her. His sons. "I do have one favor to ask of you, though."

"What?" Luke turned and blocked her way.

She nodded in the direction of the doors opening to the left. Blake's and Dalton's bedrooms. "Tell me what you see wrong."

Luke stepped into Blake's room and glanced around. Sue Ellen quickly scanned the room. She had already remade the bed and the room was immaculate. Nothing was out of place, and she hadn't done anything more in here than remake the bed. If she didn't know better, she would have sworn no eight-year-old could be using this room.

Luke frowned and walked to Dalton's room. He stepped into it and seemed to study everything. Dalton's room was an exact duplicate of Blake's, except while Blake's room had been wallpapered in red, white and blue toy soldiers, Dalton's was teddy bears. Dancing teddy bears and ABC blocks.

"I don't see anything wrong." Luke turned and faced her. "Both rooms are neat and clean. Have Blake and Dalton not been picking up their toys or something I should know about?"

"No, the boys are well trained to pick up after themselves, Luke." Personally she thought they were *too* well trained, but she didn't want to throw too much at Luke at one time. "How old is Dalton?"

"He's six, and you already knew that because you

were the one to throw the party for him." Luke's frown deepened.

"That's right. Now look at the room again, Luke. Does this look like a six-year-old boy's room to you? There are dancing teddy bears on the walls and ruffles on the yellow curtains." She was treading on dangerous ground here. Tiffany had decorated this room, and from what she had seen so far Luke had no desire to change a thing that his first wife had done. Luke had told her that she was in charge of the house and she could do what she wished with it. So far she hadn't found the courage to put his words to the test. Her gut told her that this entire house was some sort of shrine to Tiffany's memory.

"Did Dalton tell you he didn't like it? What about Blake and those toy soldiers and drums?"

"Neither boy has mentioned his room to me." She leaned against the doorjamb and watched Luke as he slowly paced across the room and then back again. His frown had turned into a scowl.

"You think they don't like their rooms?"

She might not be anyone's *real* mother, but she knew kids well enough to know that neither boy liked his room. "They don't spend any time in them, except to sleep." She shrugged. "The other week, during Dalton's party, a bunch of kids wanted to come up here and play in his room. Dalton wouldn't let them. He told them they weren't allowed upstairs, but that wasn't true because he saw me nod my permission. Dalton didn't want them to see his room, and by the look he and Blake exchanged, Blake didn't either."

"They were embarrassed?"

"I can guarantee you that none of the other boys their age have toy soldiers or dancing teddy bears up in their rooms. It was fine and cute when they were little, but your sons are growing up, Luke."

"So why haven't they said anything to me?" Luke appeared baffled yet believing.

"Maybe they're afraid."

"Afraid? Of what, me?" Now Luke sounded incredulous that his sons would be afraid of him.

"Maybe 'afraid' was the wrong word." The last thing she wanted to do was get Luke upset. "I have noticed that basically nothing has been changed in the house since their mother died." Hell, Tiffany could walk right back through the front door and pick up exactly where she left off. The only difference was, the boys were eighteen months older and Luke was now sleeping on cotton sheets. "They could be feeling that you wouldn't allow it, or that changing something she had done would be like erasing a part of her memory."

Luke ran a frustrated hand through his hair. "I guess I, I mean we, should have a talk with them tonight. Tiffany had been talking about redoing both of their rooms before she died."

Sue Ellen frowned as she backed out into the hallway. "Fine. We'll talk to them at dinner." Since Tiffany had been talking about redecorating before she lost control of her car and slammed into a telephone pole, Luke would allow her to redo the boys' rooms. It hadn't been the reason she was hoping for, but it was a start.

WIFE IN NAME ONLY

"Will you be back for lunch?" Luke usually joined her and Dalton for the noon meal. It was one of the few times during the day that she actually got to see and talk to Luke. Mostly, Dalton did all the talking, but that was okay with her. Since the wedding, Luke had been so busy outside catching up on all the work he had postponed while taking care of the boys and the house, she figured they would be celebrating their silver wedding anniversary before he had time for a quiet relaxing evening.

"Not today. The weather's turning and rain will be moving through shortly. I might as well stop at the hardware store for some supplies I need and then go over to Oliver Herr's. I hear he has a hay wagon he's looking to sell, and it's in excellent condition." Luke followed her down the stairs and into the kitchen. "I'll be home sometime this afternoon."

Luke stepped into the mudroom and pulled on his work boots. "Make sure you either take the car to the end of the drive to meet Dalton's bus, or at least an umbrella, if it's not too bad out." Luke snagged a windbreaker off the coatrack and jammed a baseball cap, advertising a tractor company, onto his head. With a preoccupied " 'Bye," Luke was gone.

She stood there and watched as he walked to his pickup. Her husband had one of those purposeful strides that carried confidence and physical strength well. His shoulders were broad and the short-sleeved shirt he had been wearing clung to his back. He looked like a farmer from the back. From the front, he looked like some movie star playing the role of a farmer. He was tanned, square-jawed and had the most incredible brown eyes with thick black lashes. A woman could drown in those eyes and go down without a whimper. Luke Walker was too darn good-looking to plow fields all day. He was also too darn sexy to live with day after day, night after night, and not have wicked thoughts.

She was having more than just wicked thoughts about his superb body as he climbed into the pickup truck and drove away. She was wondering just how thick the memories of Tiffany were that surrounded his heart.

She bit the inside of her cheek to keep any wayward tears at bay and studied the dark clouds slowly moving their way toward the farm. She hadn't doubted Luke when he said it was going to rain. The man knew his weather. But this morning the sky had been sunny, and with the warm breeze that had been blowing, the sheets she had hung out had dried quickly. The towels weren't going to be so lucky. She slipped her feet into the loafers she had kicked off earlier, stepped out back and headed for the clothesline and the still damp towels.

"Can we really pick what we want?" Blake's voice climbed an octave or two with his excitement as he flipped through pages of the wallpaper book in front of him.

Luke, who was standing by the doorway leading to his den, glanced at Sue Ellen for some help. This had been her idea to begin with; he had only carried it to the next step. While he had been at the hardware store in town earlier in the day, he had borrowed a half dozen wallpaper sample books to bring home with him.

"Within reason, Blake." Sue Ellen took his hint and smiled at the boys. "Remember, you'll have to live with the final choice for years."

"That's right, boys. We won't be changing the wallpaper like it was your underwear."

Dalton giggled and turned another page of the book in front of him. "There're so many to choose from."

"That's an understatement if I ever heard one." Sue Ellen had another book in front of her and was marveling at every new page she turned. "Another thing you can think about is painting the room instead of wallpapering it. You won't get sick of one color as fast as you would four entire walls crammed with tigers or cowboys." She tapped at a sample of a nine-inch-wide white border with green tractors and red barns. "You might also consider painting the walls and just having a border to brighten the room."

His sons crowded around Sue Ellen on the couch as she pointed out one picture after another. A flush of pleasure had brightened her complexion and added an extra sparkle in her clear blue eyes. His wife was in her element, and his sons loved having her here. He had made the right decision by asking Sue Ellen to marry him. He gave a sigh of relief. He wasn't failing his sons.

Earlier, on the way into town, he had cursed his own stupidity and blindness. How could he have been so wrapped up in the farm and his own grief and guilt that he had failed to notice his own sons' surroundings? It had taken Sue Ellen to point the problem out to him, and still he had a hard time accepting it.

Dalton was still sleeping in the same room to which he had come home from the hospital. He guessed he should be thankful that the crib had been put away and Tiffany had gone out and bought another bedroom set that matched Blake's perfectly, down to the desk with its matching hutch and chair.

Where had all the time gone?

"Dad, what do you think about this one?" Blake held up a sample containing miniature racing cars and checker flags. It would give him nightmares within two weeks, but then, what did he know about decorating? Racing cars were fine with him. At least it wasn't dancing teddy bears or pink bows. Damn, he really hated the color pink.

"Whatever you and Sue Ellen decide will be fine with me."

Tiffany had always told him he had the taste of a country hick. Making their home into some showplace hadn't been his idea of money well spent. He had much preferred the money be added to the boys' college fund, their retirement or just plain saved in case they needed it when the next drought hit. There was always a drought or too much rain. Tiffany had preferred silk wallpaper for the formal dining room or imported crystal from England. The arguments that had ensued over the years hadn't been worth the effort. Tiffany had always seemed to get her way, and he had the silk wallcovering still hanging in the dining room to prove it.

Tiffany had been gone for eighteen months now, and all he could remember were the arguments. What did that say about their marriage? What did that say about his ability to be a good husband?

"Don't you want to help the boys look through the books, Luke?" Sue Ellen sat in the middle of the couch, with one of his sons on either side of her. Thick, awkward books lay open in each of their laps. Dalton's book had to weigh more than he did, yet he didn't complain; he just kept turning the pages. His son had the same look plastered on his face as when he went through the Christmas catalog that always seemed to arrive around Halloween.

Sue Ellen was giving him that curious look again, as if she was trying to read his soul. He was beginning to hate that look. One day his new wife just might see what a black soul he had, and then what would she do?

Sue Ellen was proving to be quite a distraction. He might have made the right decision in regard to his sons, but he was now having second thoughts in regard to himself. Whatever happened to his self-control? All Sue Ellen had to do was get within six feet of him and every hormone he possessed stood up and took notice. It was a sad state of affairs, and one he planned on squashing as quickly as possible.

He glanced at his sons and Sue Ellen. "You and the boys go over the samples and see if there's anything they like. Howie, down at the hardware store, said he had another dozen or so books if you don't find anything you like in those." The last thing his overactive hormones needed was to get all cozy on the couch with Sue Ellen, even if the boys were there to act as buffers. "I've got some work to catch up on in the den. Let me know when you're ready for bed, boys, and I'll come up to say good night."

"Sure, Dad," Blake said. His son's nose was still buried in a book, so it came out all mumbly.

"See you later, Dad." Dalton lowered his gaze and immediately went back to turning the pages in his book.

Only Sue Ellen looked upset with his refusal to sit down and pore over wallpaper patterns. Well, she could just be upset. Who did she think he looked like, a combination of Ralph Lauren and Bob Vila? With a weary sigh he turned and walked away from his family.

Luke walked into the kitchen Saturday afternoon, just as Sue Ellen and the boys poured in through the front door. Overflowing shopping bags hung from every hand and were tossed onto the table with much excitement and talking. He grimaced at the sight of all those bags and mentally kissed that new hay wagon he had been thinking about buying good-bye. He had been wondering when Sue Ellen would show her natural-born instinct for the almighty shopping spree. Tiffany's sprees had been known to max out at least two of her credit cards.

"Dad, you should see all the neat stuff we got!" Blake was yanking open bags and pulling out merchandise faster than a magician pulled rabbits out of his hat.

WIFE IN NAME ONLY   85

"Dad, wait until you see what I got!" Dalton didn't want to be outdone by his older brother.

He glanced at Sue Ellen, who was smiling at his sons as they upended bags. He couldn't ever remember his sons coming home from a shopping spree with their mother, or even their grandmother, with such optimism. What in the world had Sue Ellen bought them? He frowned at the store name on all of the bags. Wright's Department Store was located on Main Street in Wild Rose. Tiffany had never shopped there. Her idea of shopping had been multilevel malls with designer stores. The closest malls had been in Sioux City, over an hour away.

"I'm afraid I got carried away and went a little overboard, but the boys are so easy to please and they did need just about everything for spring." Sue Ellen reached for the bag Blake was digging into.

Luke caught a glimpse of very feminine silk underwear, all in creamy pastels, before she jammed them back into the bag. He never knew Wright's sold sexy underwear. He took a deep breath, told himself to ignore what he had just seen and asked, "So how many credit cards did you max out?"

Sue Ellen blinked in surprise. "Ah . . . none. I didn't spend that much."

"Look, Dad. I got new sneakers and a pair of sandals." Blake ripped the lid off a shoe box and proudly showed him the white sneakers.

"I got some too, Dad!" Dalton, never to be outdone, yanked a pair of sneakers out of a box and tossed them to him. "They even have a red light in the heel that lights up every time I walk in them."

Luke pressed on the sole, and sure enough a miniature red light lit up. "They allow this in school?"

"Sure Dad, all the kids have them." Dalton reached into a pile of denim and khaki and pulled out a pair of jeans that appeared to be two sizes too big for him. "Look what else I got, baggy jeans." Dalton held up the pair of jeans and grinned. "Now they won't call me 'geek-head' in school."

Luke had a hard time swallowing the lump in his throat. "Geek-head?" Someone had been calling his son names?

"Yeah, Dad." Blake pulled a pair of khakis from the pile. "Look at mine. Sue Ellen says I look rad in them." Blake smiled at Sue Ellen as if she had just brought the sun into their lives. "You should see the shirts we got, too." Blake and Dalton started hunting through the pile. A shoe box hit the floor and a sandal slid under the table.

He was still trying to digest the geek-head remark. Who, and why, had someone called his son that name? Dalton and Blake were perfect; they weren't geek-heads.

Sue Ellen shook her head and refolded both of their pants. "I also picked up some shorts for them and a few short-sleeved tops. Spring's already here and pretty soon we'll be able to put away the sweaters and heavy socks. The boys are going to need the lighter-weight clothes to finish out the school year."

He thought about the boxes upon boxes of clothing Evelyn St. Claire had just given Dalton for his birthday and frowned. Navy blue dress slacks, white button-down shirts and a blue argyle vest. The only thing that had been missing was a bow tie, but then again, he hadn't been paying that much attention to the boxes being opened. One was probably there somewhere. There hadn't been a pair of jeans or khakis in the bunch.

"Here's my favorite, Dad, look." Blake was holding up a Hawaiian print short-sleeved shirt.

"Mine's better!" Dalton held his upside down. The parrots looked drunk.

The palm trees and brightly colored parrots would definitely brighten up the closets filled with dress shirts and designer-named sweaters. "You might need to put on sunglasses when you wear those shirts."

"Cool!" Dalton handed Sue Ellen his shirt and went back to rooting through the pile. "We didn't forget you, Dad. Sue Ellen says it wouldn't be fair if we all got something new and you didn't."

He glanced at Sue Ellen and noticed the slight flush sweeping up her cheeks. That was interesting. He only hoped she hadn't gotten him a Hawaiian shirt, too. He couldn't imagine baling hay while wearing a shirt with pineapples and palm trees printed all over it.

"Here's your bag, Dad." Blake smiled and handed him the bag.

Luke cautiously looked into the blue-and-white-striped bag. He knew everyone was watching him and tried to control his reaction. He breathed a sigh of relief when no neon colors or drunk parrots jumped out at him. A smile played across his mouth as he pulled out two pairs of the brand of jeans he always wore and two short-sleeved cotton polo shirts. One was in light blue, the other a medium shade of green. They were perfect.

He smiled at Sue Ellen. "Thank you."

"The boys helped pick them out." Sue Ellen still held Dalton's bright shirt in her hands.

By the way Blake was still clutching his shirt, Luke had a feeling he had Sue Ellen to thank for making the final decision. Wild Rose was a long way from Margaritaville. "They're just what I needed."

"See, I told you he'd like them." Blake started to arrange the clothes into two piles, his and Dalton's.

"We like shopping with Sue Ellen, Dad." Dalton climbed under the table and picked up his sandal, then added it to the box.

"Why don't you two go upstairs and put your new clothes away?" Luke ruffled each of his sons' heads as they loaded up their arms and hurried from the room. The pounding of their feet on the stairs and their laughter echoed through the house.

He turned to Sue Ellen and watched as she slowly folded each bag. "I've never seen them so excited about getting new clothes before."

"They seemed to really enjoy themselves at Wright's." One bag was neatly placed on top of another. Sue Ellen wouldn't meet his eyes. "I know the styles are a little different from what you're used to seeing them in, but all the kids dress like that nowadays."

"How did you know the kids at school were making fun of them?" He now understood the reason behind this impromptu shopping spree. Sue Ellen had known about the name calling. Why hadn't he?

WIFE IN NAME ONLY   89

Sue Ellen shrugged and carried the bags over to their storage place, next to the washing machine in the mudroom. She came back into the kitchen and opened the freezer. "What about pork chops tonight?"

He stepped next to Sue Ellen and gently closed the freezer door. "How?" He wanted an answer.

"Besides just looking at how they were dressed and the clothes that were in their closets?" Sue Ellen frowned at the refrigerator door and straightened the monthly menu of lunches served at the elementary school.

"Besides that?" Blake and Dalton were always extremely well dressed and clean. Tiffany had insisted on what she called the "classic" look and had drummed cleanliness into the boys' heads since the time they could walk. He never interfered with that lesson because he couldn't find fault with being clean.

"Well . . ." Sue Ellen turned to look out the window above the sink.

He was getting a really strange feeling in the pit of his stomach. He reached over, cupped her chin and forced her to face him. "Sue Ellen, what happened?"

"Dalton came home from school yesterday crying. It seemed a couple of kids were making fun of his clothes and calling him 'geek-head' because he didn't dress like everyone else. They said he dressed like a sissy."

"Why didn't you tell me?"

"You were busy." Sue Ellen pulled her chin out of his grasp and took a step back. "The agreement was that I handle the kids."

He felt as if someone had just sucker punched him in the gut. His son, his baby, had come home from school crying and he hadn't even known. What kind of father was he? He was failing Dalton, just like he had failed Tiffany. At least this time Sue Ellen had been there to pick up the pieces and to make things better for Dalton. For Blake too. He had to wonder how many times Blake had suffered the ridicule of his classmates and never said a word.

"You still should have told me." He had the right to know what was happening with his sons.

"What would you have done? Gone to the school and complained? That wouldn't have solved anything. It would have just made things worse for the boys."

He didn't know what he would have done, but he would have done *something*. Instead he never had the chance to make things right. Sue Ellen had taken the chance away from him, but he couldn't blame her. He had had eighteen months to make things right, and he hadn't. Sue Ellen had done exactly what he had asked her to do, handle the boys. That included their "geeky" wardrobe and problems at school.

He slowly leaned forward and brushed a kiss across Sue Ellen's brow.

"What was that for?" Sue Ellen looked startled by the simple gesture.

"For being there for him." He gave her another kiss, but this time it was against her cheek. "That was for being there for both of them." Without saying another word, he walked out of the kitchen, through the mudroom and to the barn beyond.

FIVE

Luke jumped off the tractor and stretched. The muscles in his lower back protested from being in the tractor seat for four hours straight. Work around the farm was going great, so there was no use complaining about a couple of sore muscles. He was right on schedule for the spring planting. If the weather cooperated, he was planning on a great year. He had even managed to catch up on some of the other chores he had put off after Mrs. Johnson had left to join her daughter in California. Things had never run this smoothly before. There was only one person he could thank for that miracle: his wife. Sue Ellen was an absolute dream with the boys.

He glanced toward the house as his sons' laughter reached his ears. The boys had never laughed like that before. He smiled at the carefree sound. It was music to his soul. Everything was right in the world if his sons could laugh with such joy.

Sue Ellen ran the house with confidence and a sensibility he hadn't witnessed since his mother moved to Arizona with his father. Tiffany's idea of running a smooth household was to decorate it and then complain for what seemed like twenty-four hours a day about the amount of work that always had to be done. Mrs. Johnson, the housekeeper, never complained about the boys or the amount of housework that needed to be done, but she felt it wasn't her place to make any decisions in regard to them. Every meal with Mrs. Johnson and the boys had been a headache just waiting to happen. He had been so tired of making every decision, from what to do with Blake when he refused to eat his cauliflower to whether the boys needed a haircut. After Mrs. Johnson left, things had gotten to the point where he just didn't want to get out of bed in the morning.

In the two weeks since he had been married to Sue Ellen things around the house were different. Vastly different. His sons were laughing and the house ran like a well-oiled machine. He should be jumping for joy and counting his blessings. So why did it all feel so hollow?

Sue Ellen had taken over the responsibility of his sons and the house, leaving him free to handle the farm. It had been what he wanted. It had been their agreement. So why was he missing his own family? Why did it feel like he was standing on the outside and all the love and warmth was on the inside? It was very disconcerting to have exactly what you wanted and then realize it wasn't what you wanted after all.

So what exactly did he want? It was a damn good question. One he didn't have an answer for.

He headed for the side of the house, from where all the laughter and shrieks were coming. Right now he wanted to see what was so amusing. He turned the corner and came to a complete halt.

Sue Ellen and the boys were turning over the plot of ground his mother had used for a small kitchen garden. Tiffany had taken one look at the small fenced-in plot and yanked out the vegetables and planted rosebushes. The roses hadn't faired too well. Out of the dozen or so bushes Tiffany had planted, only one or two were still alive. Sue Ellen had already replanted the two survivors in a nice, neat spot on the outside of the fenced area.

Inside the picket fence was another story. It was a disaster. A huge, muddy disaster with Sue Ellen and the boys right in the middle.

Luke leaned against the house and studied his family. Were those two little mud balls the same boys who used to cry if so much as a speck of dirt landed on them? Their jeans were streaked with mud and their work boots were so caked with the stuff that if someone threw them into a river they would surely drown. He was having a hard time trying to figure out how they were even managing to walk, let alone work a shovel into the soil. Maybe that was what was so funny. Blake and Dalton were so busy laughing at each other and themselves that none of the work was getting done.

He glanced at Sue Ellen. The woman was attacking the ground as if it was her mortal enemy. There was a smile plastered across her face, or at least he thought it was a smile. Sue Ellen had so much dirt smeared across her face, it was hard to tell. What in the world had she been doing? It not only appeared as if she had been making mud pies all morning, but eating them as well.

If Sue Ellen had bothered to ask, he would have told her to wait a couple more days for the soil in this particular spot to dry out, before turning it over. Heck, if she had asked, he would have turned it over for her. He would love to see the vegetable garden back. There was something about biting into a just-picked tomato that was still warm from the sun. But his wife hadn't asked for his opinion or his help. She never did. Sue Ellen had to be the most independent woman in the entire state of Iowa. Why hadn't he noticed that trait before?

She also was the sexiest woman he'd ever met, and he'd be damned if he could figure out how she did it. Even now, covered in mud and looking like something a cat wouldn't even drag in, he wanted her. Sue Ellen never flaunted herself in front of him, or any other man. His gut reaction was that she hadn't the foggiest notion of exactly how sexy she was. Take right now, for instance.

Sue Ellen was wearing a pair of tight jeans and his black rubber boots, which were obviously three sizes too big for her small feet. He could see the high collar of a red turtleneck and some flannel shirt all peaking out from under a huge, baggy navy sweatshirt that had one of the Seven Dwarfs on the front and hung almost to her knees. To top off this lovely ensemble, she had yanked on one of his baseball caps, advertising a seed company. She had pulled her long silky ponytail through the opening in the back. Covered with mud, she should have been the most unappealing woman in the county. Instead he stood there achingly hard with desire. His fantasy was to undress her layer by enticing layer and make hard and fast love to her against the shower wall.

At first when his dormant hormones woke up and took notice of the woman who had become his wife, he had chucked it off as a natural process, and that any woman—any female body—would have received the same attention. It was a blatant lie, told to himself by a man who desperately wanted to believe it. It was a lie he couldn't believe any longer. He wanted Sue Ellen, not just any woman.

He wanted the one woman he couldn't have. He wanted his wife.

"Hey, Dad!" Blake was the first one to notice him standing there propping up the house with his shoulder. "We're helping Sue Ellen make a garden."

"Yeah, Dad," shouted Dalton. "Sue Ellen says we can even get to pick some of the stuff we're going to plant."

"I chose carrots," Blake shouted.

"I'm choosing peas." Dalton jammed his shovel into the soil about an inch and flipped over a clump of dirt about the size of a pancake.

He pushed away from the house and held his chuckle as Sue Ellen grunted and turned over another shovel full. Even with the slight nip in the air, her face had a sheen of perspiration coating it. The desire burning in his gut flamed hotter. He wanted to make Sue Ellen sweat, but shovels weren't part of the fantasy. He wanted to make her groan and moan and sweetly scream her release.

He didn't feel like chuckling now. He felt like howling in frustration. Lord, how had she done this to him, when she hadn't so much as looked in his direction?

"Hey, Dad, what's your choice? Sue Ellen says even you get a choice." Blake turned over a pancake-sized clump of dirt of his own.

He didn't even have to think about his answer. "Tomatoes."

"You can't pick tomatoes, Dad," Dalton said. "Sue Ellen already did."

He glanced at Sue Ellen, and she gave him a smile that went directly to his gut. "Sorry, but I love biting into a just-picked tomato that's still warm from the sun." His gaze followed her small pink tongue as it slid across her lower lip like she was tasting the succulent fruit right this very minute. "I love how the juice just explodes into your mouth and runs down your chin."

His gaze slid from her temptingly moist lower lip to her chin as he envisioned kissing the path the sweet juice would take. He wanted to be the one to lick away any juice that trailed its way down her chin, or any other part of her body. Lord, what he wouldn't give to get Sue Ellen alone with a bushel basket filled with tomatoes.

He blinked away the fantasy and noticed the strange look Sue Ellen was giving him. Lord, he hoped his thoughts weren't readable. Sue Ellen would be running for the hills and crying *foul* the entire way. And he wouldn't blame her. It wasn't fair to change the rules in the middle of the game. Taking

Sue Ellen to bed would be one hell of a change. He had promised her that she would be a wife in name only. He had been the one to come right out and say they wouldn't be sharing a bed. A shower stall might not be a bed technically, but it would amount to the same thing. Sex. Hot, sweet sex.

"Dad?"

He shook his head and turned toward his older son. "What, Blake?" Was that his voice sounding all rough and husky?

"Didn't you hear me?"

"Hear what?" Now Sue Ellen, Blake and Dalton were all giving him that concerned look, as if they might be thinking about calling the men with the little white coats, known as straitjackets. He didn't blame them. Could a person self-commit himself for lusting after his own wife?

"I asked what else you wanted besides tomatoes."

He wanted Sue Ellen, and the hell with the tomatoes. He wanted his damn hormones to go take another long vacation. He wanted a hell of a lot of things he obviously wasn't going to get. "Peppers."

"What kind of peppers?" Sue Ellen positioned her shovel and then applied the weight of her foot. The blade of the shovel went about halfway in. With a silent huff of air she turned the dirt over.

"Bell peppers." He couldn't stand to see the struggle any longer. Barely half the garden was turned, and none of that was turned properly. He walked around the fence and entered through the swinging gate. Sometime this summer, when he had a free moment, the fence would need another coat of paint.

He mentally added it to the endless list of chores already stored in his head. "The kind of peppers you make stuffed peppers from."

"You like stuffed peppers?" Sue Ellen watched as he took the shovel from Blake and started to turn over the garden.

"Yeah." Blake and Dalton took his entrance into the garden as a signal to leave. Both boys ran toward the tree house he had built for them last summer. Huge mud balls went flying off their boots as they sprinted and laughed their way across the yard.

It was good to see the boys enjoying themselves. It had been a long time since he had seen them this happy, if ever. Blake and Dalton were changing right before his eyes. Changing for the better. Blake was becoming more outspoken and confident. Dalton was allowing Luke to disappear from his sight for more than five minutes at a time before he came looking for him. Ever since his mother had died, Dalton had clung to him. He understood the separation anxiety and had made allowances for it. Getting Dalton started in kindergarten had been a real challenge, but he had managed. These current changes he couldn't take credit for. Sue Ellen was the motivating force behind them.

"Do you know how to make stuffed peppers?" He turned shovelful after shovelful. The soil was still a nice dark color, a testament to years of composting by his mother. "The ground is going to need some manure."

Sue Ellen frowned at the soil beneath her feet. "Oh."

"Is that 'oh,' you don't know how to make stuffed peppers, or an 'oh' about shoveling manure?" He flashed her a grin but continued turning shovelfuls of soil.

"The peppers are easy; it's the manure I'm worried about." Sue Ellen turned another shovelful and then glanced at the dirt he had just turned. "Where does one purchase manure?"

"From someone with a lot of animals." He couldn't keep the chuckle out of his voice. Sue Ellen looked about as enthused about spreading manure as he would about going to get a root canal. He had to take pity on his poor wife; after all, she would be the one making him the stuffed peppers. The one thing he had learned after Mrs. Johnson left was that his culinary talents were basically nonexistent. Unless those stuffed peppers came in little frozen cardboard boxes with microwave directions, he wasn't getting any. "I'll make you a deal. I'll turn in the manure and get this garden ready for you to plant if you whip up some stuffed peppers whenever it's convenient for you."

"Deal." Sue Ellen apparently didn't have to think twice about it. Another shovelful went over. "How come the field you were turning this morning wasn't this wet?"

"Higher ground. It drains quicker." He hadn't known she had been watching him this morning. "There's about a day or two difference in how quickly this will dry out. It will also depend on how much rain we have and how hard the sun is working."

"The top couple of inches were dry, but once we started to dig, it got wet."

"That's good. You'll want soil that can hold the moisture, yet still drain eventually. The problem around here is usually not enough rain, not too much rain." The one subject he knew about was farming. He didn't feel awkward talking to Sue Ellen about drainage or manure. Every other subject seemed to tie up his tongue. He wasn't real comfortable talking to his own wife yet. He needed to practice more, and this seemed like the perfect time. "If you're going to really get into gardening and all, you might want to consider starting a compost pile."

"I don't know, Luke." Sue Ellen frowned at her shovel and refused to meet his gaze. "I might not be any good at this kind of thing. I had a couple of houseplants once. I managed to kill them off one by one."

He bit the inside of his cheek to keep from laughing. Sue Ellen looked guilty as hell for knocking off a couple of philodendrons or whatever it was she had. "Composting is as easy as taking out the garbage. I'll be around to give you pointers if you need them."

"You're so busy now. I don't want to impose on your time." Sue Ellen flipped over the shovelful of dirt. "How hard can it be to grow a tomato plant or two?"

He had to wonder if he had just been put in his proper place. He had offered to help, and had been turned down flat. Politely, but flat. Granted, he hadn't been offering Sue Ellen a whole bunch of advice or help since their wedding, but he had a reason for that. He had wanted to see how well Sue Ellen handled the house and the kids before he had to step in. So far he hadn't stepped in once, which was a relief, yet a disappointment. He had thought to enjoy the reprieve, and he had, for the first couple of days. Now it was beginning to feel as if his family didn't need him at all. They needed the income the farm brought in, but not him personally.

His shovel bit into the dirt with more force than necessary. "It's not that hard, but if you have any questions ask me. The garden will be for my family, after all."

"Our." Sue Ellen's voice was barely a whisper and he had trouble hearing her.

"What?"

Sue Ellen's shoulders went back and her chin, the one he had been fantasizing about, went up a good inch or two. "I said *our.* The garden is for our family, not just yours."

As her words registered, the shovel nearly slipped out of his hands. He glanced from the stubborn tilt of her chin to the tree house, where Blake and Dalton were sitting side by side discussing something. Soon the buds that were just forming would turn into leaves and he wouldn't be able to see them behind the thick foliage. "You're right, Sue Ellen. It's our family. Together we are making it one."

Sue Ellen stared at him for a moment before turning her back and continuing digging. "Sorry about snapping. It's a touchy subject, that's all."

"Why?"

"Why what?"

"Why's it a touchy subject?" He continued digging because Sue Ellen was. She was obviously more relaxed when her hands were busy, and besides, the garden was nearly done. "Someone in town been giving you a hard time?" He might spend practically every waking hour on the farm, but occasionally he did stop in town, and lately the rumor mill had been going full force. So much so that quite a few people had enlightened him on the latest rumors concerning his and Sue Ellen's hurried marriage. The consensus was that Sue Ellen was carrying his child. He had hotly denied the rumors, but had only received knowing grins in return. He had decided not to defend their marriage and let people think what they wanted to think. It would be obvious to all that Sue Ellen wasn't pregnant as the months went by.

"Not really."

"So why so touchy? I'm sorry for the slip, but we've only been a family for two weeks now. I'll get the hang of this 'our' stuff soon"—he gave her what he hoped was a beguiling smile—"promise."

Sue Ellen's smile didn't contain its usual warmth. "It does take some getting used to, doesn't it?"

"Having problems adjusting?" He leaned on his shovel and studied the woman who had become his wife to protect his sons. He hadn't noticed her having a hard time adjusting. In fact the total opposite had seemed true. Sue Ellen didn't just fall into motherhood, she bloomed into the role. He had to wonder if she was regretting marrying him.

"No." This time her smile was a little more honest. "It's just little things." Sue Ellen glanced across the yard to where the boys were sitting. "Like the other day, I was in town picking up some groceries when I ran into Thelma. She wanted to know how Luke's boys were. It's the same with just about everyone. It's the same three questions. 'How's marriage treating you? How's Luke? How are Luke's boys?'" Sue Ellen kept her gaze on the boys.

"There's a rumor going around that I'm pregnant, and that's why you married me."

"I heard it, denied it without too much result, so I just let it slide. They'll figure it out sooner or later." If he hadn't been studying her profile so closely, he wouldn't have noticed the blush sweeping up her face. Sue Ellen was embarrassed. The town was trashing her reputation, and he was letting it slide . . . some husband he was. "Want me to go to town and straighten out a few chosen people on that subject?"

Sue Ellen shook her head. "No, but thanks. The ones spreading the rumors will be the ones looking like fools in a couple of months." Sue Ellen wiped her forearm across her forehead, leaving behind another smear of dirt. "More than one person said to me that soon we would be starting our own family, and things would work out just fine. I can't understand what's worse, that people just assume Blake and Dalton are yours and any child we would have together would be ours, or that things weren't fine already." Sue Ellen shook her head and went back to digging the last few feet. "I don't remember saying or doing anything that would lead people to believe things weren't fine right now."

He now had a better understanding of what was

upsetting her. The people of Wild Rose were normally generous and kindhearted, but sometimes their hearts took the wrong path. "A lot of people were, let's say, shocked at the speed of our wedding and jumped to their own conclusions. Add to that the fact that most people around here marry young and stay with the same partner throughout life. Divorce in Wild Rose is still a scandalous event. Most people around here couldn't imagine marrying someone who already came with a family of his own, so they're applying their thoughts to your life, Sue Ellen. Everyone around town still considers Blake and Dalton Tiffany's boys, and it will just take some time for them to adjust to the fact that they have a new mother."

"So it's not me having a hard time adjusting, it's the town?" Sue Ellen appeared to be thinking this over.

"I think you adjusted beautifully. The boys adore you and I'm your humblest servant since tasting your fried chicken and biscuits."

Sue Ellen laughed. "Spoken like a true man, but I thank you anyway." With one last shovelful, she finished her corner of the garden plot.

He finished up his and met her at the gate. "There's one more element to the hassle the town's been giving you, Sue Ellen."

"What's that?"

"Evelyn." He allowed her to precede him through the gate, and then he closed it behind them. "From the few times she has talked to me since the wedding, she hasn't adjusted to this at all. She could be one of the ones stirring up rumors in town."

Sue Ellen sadly shook her head. "Why would she want her grandsons surrounded by rumors?"

"Evelyn's still grieving for Tiffany." He gave a sharp whistle, and both of the boys scrambled down the ladder and were running toward them. "Don't underestimate her, Sue Ellen. She still wants the boys."

Sue Ellen frowned as her family entered the mudroom. Most of her thoughts were on what Luke had just told her out in the garden, but the rest of them were on her family, her mud-coated family. Lord, she hoped she didn't look as bad as the boys. One glance down at the front of her crushed those hopes. She wasn't quite as muddy as the boys, but she came in a close second. Luke was the only clean one there, once he took off his mud-caked boots, that is.

She looked at the boys and shook her head. "You two aren't walking through the house looking like that." She kicked off the pair of Luke's boots that she had borrowed and opened the lid to the washing machine. "Make sure there's nothing in your pockets and then strip down to your skivies. Toss your dirty clothes right in the washer and then head upstairs for a nice warm shower."

"Who gets to go first?" Blake dumped his jacket and his sweatshirt into the washer and was working on his jeans.

She helped Dalton pull his sweatshirt over his head

and gave it a toss. She glanced at both of their faces and hands and shook her head. "You can shower together, but I don't want any fooling around in there." White teeth flashed behind muddy faces.

Dalton stepped out of his jeans and handed them to her. "What about you? You're covered in mud, too."

"I'm not quite as bad as you and Blake, so I can wait until you're done with your shower before I have mine." She tossed Dalton's jeans into the washer. "Socks, too."

She lifted her own dirty sweatshirt over her head and added it to the machine. She noticed that Luke had hung up his jacket and removed his boots. He was leaning against the wall in the doorway that led into the kitchen. Not a speck of dirt touched his clothes, and he had a silly grin spread across his face as he watched them all undress.

"Sue Ellen can use my shower while you two are in the other one." Luke cocked an eyebrow at her and gave a low chuckle.

"What about your jeans, Sue Ellen?" Blake stood in front of her frowning. He was dressed only in a white T-shirt and underwear. "They have mud all over them."

She didn't have to look at Luke to know his smile had grown. He was just waiting to see how she would get out of this one. Fine, she'd show him. That laugh of his held a little bit too much challenge to suit her. "You're absolutely right, Blake."

The old flannel shirt she had on used to be her father's. On her it hung to midthigh and was soft and faded from many washings. She turned her back, unsnapped her jeans and stepped out of them. The most anyone could see were her legs. She wasn't indecent, and she refused to be embarrassed at taking off her pants in front of Luke. She had shorts that showed more leg and a bathing suit that showed a heck of a lot more. She yanked off her socks and dropped them into the machine. "Come on, boys, I'll start that shower for you."

She brushed past Luke and gave him a quick glance beneath her lashes to see his reaction. He wasn't laughing any longer. He appeared to be in pain. Well, hell, wasn't that just great. She frowned and muttered as she followed the boys up the steps. The first time she drops her pants for her husband and he acts as if he's in pain at the mere sight of her legs. So much for any desire he might have been hiding from her. She didn't think her legs were that bad. Hell, she had even shaved them last night.

Luke entered the family room and quietly sat in the leather recliner. His chair. Sue Ellen favored the overstuffed couch, where she was curled up in one corner, watching some movie on television. Ten minutes earlier they had tucked the boys into bed. It was now a nightly tradition in the Walker household. Every night the boys wanted both him and Sue Ellen to tuck them in. It was a nice tradition.

Tonight he was breaking what had become a habit. Every night since their wedding, after the boys were all tucked in, he had disappeared into his office to catch up on paperwork, reading or the local farm report. He had left Sue Ellen alone so she could have some quiet time and some privacy. Tonight he'd brought a couple of magazines here to read while she watched TV. Their being in the same room, relaxing and enjoying the evening, had more of a family feel to it.

He wanted to start feeling like he was part of this family again.

He liked Sue Ellen's company. The more he was in it, the more he learned about the woman who had become his wife. She was the most independent woman he'd ever run across, yet she had a sense of humor that appealed to him. Her heart was as big as the entire state, and she was totally in love with his sons. She cooked like a dream and never whined or complained. She was the perfect woman, right down to those incredibly long, satiny smooth legs. When she had dropped her jeans in the mudroom earlier that afternoon he had nearly had heart failure.

He had seen Sue Ellen's legs before. Heck, he'd been seeing them since he was five and they were in kindergarten together. Over the years she had been out to the farm for plenty of the barbeques Tiffany loved to throw. He had noticed her legs before, but he wasn't prepared for her to slide down that raspy zipper and step out of her jeans like that. He never thought she would take the challenge. Sue Ellen had once again proved him wrong. There was something about those smooth, silky thighs and the way that flannel shirt had brushed against them that had sent his blood pressure soaring and his hormones on a rampage.

It had taken him a good half an hour before he was able to come into the house and act as if nothing had happened. Something had happened, though. He'd discovered he was in lust with his wife.

"Did you want to watch something else?" Sue Ellen turned from the television as a commercial blared on about a new pickup truck that was like a rock.

"No." He held up a magazine that was still sitting unopened on his lap. "I was going to catch up on some reading." *And stare at my wife.*

Sue Ellen reached for the remote. "Let me turn it down some, then."

"No, you don't have to. It isn't bothering me." He glanced over at the doorway as Dalton came hesitantly into the room. "What's wrong, Dalt?"

Sue Ellen quickly jumped up from the couch and ran over to the boy. "Are you feeling all right?" Luke smiled at the motherly reaction.

"Yes." Dalton allowed Sue Ellen to press the back of her hand against his forehead. "I need to ask you something."

"Me?" Sue Ellen backed away and sat back down. Dalton sat next to her on the couch.

"I'm not sure." Dalton nervously plucked at his Star Wars pajamas.

"Not sure about what to ask, or who to ask?" Luke placed the magazine on the end table and leaned forward. He hadn't seen Dalton this upset in a long time.

"I know what, but I don't know if I have to ask you first, or Sue Ellen."

"How about if you tell us both what's on your mind, Dalton." He glanced at Sue Ellen, who looked upset just seeing Dalton upset. Great; now he had two to contend with. "Sue Ellen and I won't mind which one you ask first. Right, Sue Ellen?"

"Right." Sue Ellen reached out and ruffled Dalton's hair. "What's the problem?"

Dalton looked ready to cry. Huge tears were pooling in his big blue eyes. "Can I call Sue Ellen 'Mom,' instead of Sue Ellen? All the kids in my class have a mom except me."

"You want to call me Mom?" Sue Ellen's voice sounded as if she had just swallowed a mouthful of glass. It was all rough and broken up.

"Billy Strong says you can't be our homeroom mom next year in first grade cause you ain't my real mom." Dalton brushed at a tear silently rolling down his cheek with the back of his hand. "He says since I call you Sue Ellen, you can't be my mom. Moms are called Mom."

"So you want to call me Mom just so I can be your homeroom mom next year?" Sue Ellen's voice broke on nearly every other word.

"No." Dalton looked over at Luke. "You said Sue Ellen will be our new mom."

"Yes, I did, and she *is* your new mom." Tears were already forming in the back of his throat and Luke had no idea how much longer he would be able to hold out against them. "I also told you that if you felt uncomfortable calling her mom, you didn't have to. The decision would be up to you." He and Sue Ellen had already discussed that before the wedding.

Dalton nodded. "I really want to call her Mom, because she's the best mom in the whole wide world."

Sue Ellen reached for Dalton and pulled him into a hug that threatened to cut off his supply of oxygen. "I'll be honored if you want to call me Mom, Dalton." Sue Ellen's voice shattered on every word, but he and Dalton knew what she was saying.

Dalton pulled back and said, "Cool." Then he gave her a big grin. "Mom."

Sue Ellen laughed such a carefree laugh that Luke felt as if his heart was going to explode from the sheer joy of it. Dalton's laughter joined hers. He watched in awe as his son and wife melted into a pile of arms, legs and tickles. A few minutes later Dalton was crying "Uncle," and Sue Ellen was deemed the winner.

"Come on, Dalton, I'll tuck you back into your bed." He stood up and walked over to the couch.

Dalton stood up and reached for his hand. "Okay." Dalton turned to Sue Ellen. "Good night, Mom."

Sue Ellen's hand was visibly trembling when she ruffled Dalton's hair and whispered, "Good night, son."

Dalton grinned and then proceeded to pull Luke out of the family room. He kept glancing over his shoulder at Sue Ellen. Her gaze was following his, tears were streaming down her face and she had the most beautiful smile on her face. She looked like someone who had just been handed the world.

* * *

Five minutes later Luke returned to the family room. Dalton had taken a couple of moments to calm down and to be reassured that Sue Ellen would definitely want to be his homeroom mom next year. The television was off and Sue Ellen was standing in front of the big picture window staring off into the night.

"Do you know, from this viewpoint you can't see any lights at all out there. It's like we're the only ones here. I've never seen the night so dark before." Sue Ellen's voice sounded much calmer. Thankfully the tears had dried. He never knew what to do with a crying woman.

He walked over and stood next to her. "You've lived in town your entire life. There's always some light shining, or the distant sounds of other people coming and going. Out here it's a different world."

"It's soothing."

He'd never heard it put quite like that before, but he had to agree. The silence agreed with him. Sue Ellen agreed with him. He moved closer just so he could smell the fruity scent of her shampoo. "In the summer months you can sit out back on the deck and hear nothing but the insects calling to one another."

"Heaven surrounded by cornfields."

"Something like that." He was quiet as he scanned the darkness beyond the window. He wondered what Sue Ellen was staring at. Nothing caught his eye, because there was nothing out there to see. He turned to Sue Ellen. "You handled Dalton wonderfully tonight."

"Dalton doesn't need handling." Sue Ellen reached up and started to pull the drapes closed.

He stopped her. His big hand covered her smaller one, and he could feel her trembling. He gently squeezed her fingers. Why was she so nervous? Was it him, or was it just the aftershock of Dalton's visit? He gave her a reassuring smile. "You're a natural-born mother, Sue Ellen."

"What's that supposed to mean?" Sue Ellen jerked her hand out from under his.

"It means you have the heart of a mother. Some women don't, you know." Why was she acting so defensively? He was paying her one of the highest compliments he could think of and she was acting as if he had just insulted her. "You should have been surrounded by children, lots of children."

He watched in confusion as every ounce of color drained from her face. Pain and sadness filled her eyes, only to be swept away by tears that overflowed and ran down her pale cheeks.

"What's wrong?" He moved toward her, only to have her step back, out of his reach. Those tears were ripping apart his heart, drop by precious drop.

"Nothing's wrong, Luke. It's late and I'm tired." Sue Ellen backed up a few steps and ducked her head. "If you'll excuse me, I'll see you in the morning."

He stood there in shock as she fled the room. His wife had actually fled his company in tears. What in the world was going on? One moment she was bursting with happiness because Dalton was going to be calling her "Mom" from now on, and the next she was running from the room. Why was there such pain and sadness in her beautiful blue eyes when he mentioned what a natural mother she was? Why was she crying?

Sue Ellen had to know she was a good mother. Dalton had just told her that she was the best mother in the whole world, and his child never lied. He, himself, had just complimented her on her mother's heart. It wasn't making sense. Sue Ellen wasn't making sense.

Unless . . . unless she really did want a child of her own but had given up the dream to marry him and to raise his sons.

They weren't his sons any longer. Blake and Dalton were now *their* sons. Sue Ellen had made them all one family. She had given him his dream. She deserved to have a dream of her own come true. He wouldn't mind a daughter, or another son, for that matter.

Maybe he had been a little too hasty when he had told Sue Ellen she would be his wife in name only. Hasty—hell, he had been out of his mind. It was his only excuse, temporary insanity. What else could have been his reason for making such an asinine statement? Wife in name only! He had never heard of such a load of manure in his life.

He wanted his wife in his bed.

SIX

Sue Ellen stood back, stretched the kinks out of her back and surveyed three days of hard work. She studied the kitchen with a critical eye for detail. Her final verdict was a nine out of a possible ten. The light above the kitchen table wasn't to her taste, and the recess lighting above the counters was a tad too modern, but she could live with that now that the rest of the room was livable. She smiled and rolled her head, easing the cramp in her neck. The kitchen was more than just livable; it was now hers.

She hadn't realized what a possessive streak she had until she started living in Tiffany's frilly, fussy house. The kitchen had had wonderful basics, thanks probably to Luke's mother and not his first wife. Tiffany would have never installed such timeless classics. The cabinets were pine and varnished to a high gloss. The floor was random pine and the countertops were a near-white granite. The appliances were white and in excellent condition.

The rest of the room had held the overbearing touch of Tiffany. The cabinets had boasted huge, gaudy brass knobs. The walls had been papered in a pink cabbage rose design and the four chairs around the pine kitchen table had matching cushions. Miniblinds and a matching pleated valance obscured the huge picture window. The three stools at the counter had been a true horror. The total effect had been overwhelming and out of balance with the farmhouse. It hadn't cost her a lot, besides time and sweat, to strip the wallpaper and the gaudy trimmings.

The top half of the room was now painted a crisp white and the bottom a pale springtime green. A wallpaper border of herbs separated the two colors. White porcelain knobs graced the cabinets and green checkered valances were the only coverings on the windows. Her grandmother's antique secretary desk had found a home against one of the walls and was now filled with Luke's mother's cookbooks, which she had located in the attic when she was putting some stuff up there to store. She had used some of the money from the sale of her own furniture to purchase a nice-size area rug for under the table and three plain pine stools for the counter. Her mother had given her three potted herbs for the windowsill above the kitchen sink, along with instructions on how to care for them.

She frowned at the herbs as she reached up to rub at a knot in the back of her neck. For the past two days, the parsley had been looking slightly wilted, but she was praying that was from the shock of moving or the paint fumes. Her mother could grow an oak tree from a splinter, while she could kill a redwood just by walking past it.

WIFE IN NAME ONLY 117

She jerked in surprise as her hand was pushed aside and a pair of strong masculine hands took their place at the nape of her neck. She hadn't heard Luke enter the house. He must have come in through the back door in his office.

Luke's voice was a low rumble. "Here, let me." The pad of his thumb pressed on the knot and gently rubbed. "I told you to take it easy. You're doing too much."

The heat and the strength of his fingers sent a shiver of need rushing through her body. "It's only a kink." She could have worked it out herself, but Luke's hands felt too wonderful, too tempting to push away. Her husband never touched her, unless it was by accident. This wasn't an accident.

"I told you that I would paint the kitchen for you, but you didn't listen, or you just couldn't wait. I'm not sure which."

She moved her ponytail out of his way and glanced over her shoulder at her husband. "I don't mind painting, Luke." His brown eyes seemed darker and full of mystery. She wondered what he was thinking at that very moment. It certainly couldn't be what was running through her own mind. "You have enough work to do with the farm and all."

"The same could be said for you, Sue Ellen. You have enough to do with the kids and the house and all." Long fingers brushed at the short, fine hairs at the nape of her neck that were too short to be gathered in her usual ponytail. His eyes darkened to nearly black.

Her breath caught in her throat at the heat in his

eyes and the slow caress. She told herself she was just imagining it all. Luke couldn't possibly desire her. "The kitchen is part of the house."

Luke's gaze went back to her neck and shoulders. "Relax, or I'm never going to be able to work this knot out."

She turned back around and tried to do as he asked, but it was impossible. She would never be able to relax as long as he was touching her. The knot was going to be permanently adhered to her neckbone in another minute. She bit her lip as he pressed and kneaded the knot. "So, how do you like the kitchen now?" Luke had given his permission for her to do whatever it was she wanted to do to the room. But giving permission and actually seeing the results were two different things. She had purposely set out to erase every sign of Tiffany from the kitchen and put her own mark on the room. She had succeeded, but maybe it was too much, too soon.

"I like it." Luke's fingers kneaded her shoulders for a minute and then went back to work on the stubborn knot. "It doesn't look so . . . busy."

She let out the breath she had been holding and relaxed. Luke actually liked it! "Thank you." *Busy* had been a very polite way of describing the room before she had gotten her hands on it. She had to wonder what Luke had told Tiffany after she had finished decorating it, and then forced that thought away. She was doing what she had promised herself she wouldn't do. She had been comparing herself to Tiffany. A futile endeavor if ever she heard one. No one could compare favorably against the perfect

WIFE IN NAME ONLY

memory of Luke's first wife, so why even bother? Tiffany was no longer here; she *was*.

Sue Ellen rotated her head and felt the knot that had been there for two days melt away under Luke's fingers. Lord, the man had magic hands.

Luke's fingers gentled into a light caress and she felt her stomach contract and her breasts grow heavy with need. A breath stirred the fine hairs on the back of her neck and her nipples actually ached and hardened. She closed her eyes and allowed the need to wash over her. Luke was so close, she could feel the heat of his body and the exhalation of his every breath. She wanted nothing more than to lean back into his hardness and feel his hands work their magic on the rest of her body. The daydream pulled her closer. She could almost touch the fantasy.

Her name came on a hoarse whisper close to her ear, followed by a soft brushing against her neck. She jumped and turned as if someone had just fired a gun. "What?" A fiery blush was heating her face, but she prayed Luke wouldn't notice. "Did you say something?" Lord, what had she been doing?

Luke gave her a peculiar look and slowly dropped his hands to his sides as he studied her face and shook his head. His eyes, which had always been a nice, deep brown, were nearly black and the color in his cheeks seemed heightened. "I'll go meet Dalton's bus." Without saying another word, he turned and walked out the front door.

Sue Ellen gulped in another breath and thought hard as her racing heart continued to pound against her breast. She had imagined it, hadn't she? Luke hadn't whispered her name with such need, had he? His lips hadn't brushed her neck, had they? What if they had and she had jumped away from him as if someone had just dumped a bucket of ice water over her head? Lord, she didn't know!

How could that be? Was she that flustered that she could no longer tell reality from a daydream? Her nights were tortured by dreams of making hot, slow love with Luke, but this was the middle of the day. Luke had been staring at her as if . . . as if what? She wanted to say as if she were stark, raving nuts, but that wasn't true. Her husband had been staring at her mouth as if he had wanted to kiss it. No, that wasn't right either. Luke had been staring at her mouth as if he had wanted to devour it.

Lord, she *was* losing her mind.

She walked across the kitchen and glanced at the refrigerator door as she passed it. Blake's math paper, with an A and a gold star, was proudly displayed, along with one of Dalton's drawings. A smile tugged at her mouth as she studied Dalton's picture of his family. Two adult stick figures and two smaller stick figures took up a good portion of the white construction paper. The rest of the paper was taken up by what she had assumed was a horse but had turned out to be a dog. A big brown dog of questionable origin. Dalton wanted a dog and wasn't being shy about his desire.

Would his father be shy about his?

With a frown she stared out the window as Luke slowly made his way down the driveway. His hands were shoved into the pockets of his jeans and a stiff breeze was molding his shirt to his back. Luke hadn't bothered with a coat. Either he had forgotten how chilly it was outside, or he had been in too much of a hurry to leave the kitchen and her company.

She bit her lower lip and refused to give in to the tears threatening to spill as she turned away from the window and the view of her husband's back in the distance. Luke never forgot about the weather. His life's work depended on him knowing about it. She never had to turn on the local radio station to get a weather report on how to dress the boys; she just asked her husband. Luke knew what the temperature would be within two degrees.

Luke had left the house without a coat because he didn't want to be in her company for the extra moment it would have taken to grab a jacket from the mudroom. So, either the desire she had been feeling had been plastered across her face like a neon sign, or he had really wanted to kiss her and she had acted like some Victorian virgin who had just lost her chaperone.

She didn't know which would be worse.

Sue Ellen parked in front of The Mane on Main and got out of the car. She had an hour before Dalton was finished with school for the day and Stella had fit her in for a quick trim. Stella not only cut hair wonderfully, but she was nice enough not to spend her day gossiping about other people's problems. Stella was the only stylist who worked her scissors faster than she worked her mouth. The only drawback with The Mane was that it was gossip central. Whatever went on in town, or even in the county, was heard there first. The only other establishment to give it a run for the money was Nick's Barber Shop, three stores down. Luke had gone to Nick's for a haircut yesterday and had returned in a quiet, strange mood. The rumors about their hasty wedding and her nonexistent pregnancy must still be flying around town.

Sue Ellen knew she was in for a real fun time for the next forty minutes. Common sense told her to stay clear of the shop and trim her own hair, but two things prevented her from taking her own advice. First, she wanted to deny the rumors that she was pregnant, and the best place to do that was at The Mane. Second, every time she tried to trim her own hair it ended up crooked.

With a steady breath, she opened the door and stepped inside the lion's den. Every woman in the place turned and stared at her.

"Sue Ellen you're here." Stella came hurrying forward.

She hung up her coat and followed Stella to the row of sinks at the back of the shop. "Yep, that's me. Right on time." A couple of people nodded to her as she passed. She slowly sank into a chair as Stella snapped a plastic sheet around her neck. "Nice crowd today."

Stella pumped up the chair and tilted it back. "You don't know the half of it." Stella turned on the water full force and tested it.

Sue Ellen closed her eyes as Stella's fingers worked

a fruity-scented shampoo through her hair. "I'm not sure if I want to know." The looks she had received had been more curious than condemning. Not a gaze in the shop had zeroed in on her stomach to gauge and measure. Strange.

Five minutes later she was seated in Stella's little cubical. With a row of hair dyers blowing directly behind them and empty chairs on either side of them, there was a smidgen of privacy, if they kept their voices down. "Give it to me, Stella. What's the word?" She hadn't actually received a cold shoulder when she had come in, but the temperature had lowered a few degrees. Why?

"There was a rumor that you were pregnant, but Luke seems to have killed that one."

A blush was threatening to climb up her face. Great; what in the world did he say, "I never slept with my wife after the ceremony, let alone before it"? "He's right, I'm not pregnant."

Stella tugged a comb through her long hair and studied the ends. In a voice loud enough to reach a perked ear or two, she said, "Not too many splits. I'm thinking no more than an inch or two." Stella's voice lowered. "I never thought you were."

Sue Ellen nodded as Stella started to pile her hair on top of her head with huge plastic clips. "So what's the rumor now? How did I manage to trick Luke into marrying me?"

"No one seems to know, but there's some interesting speculation going around." Stella picked up her scissors and started to cut about an inch off the bottom of her hair. Stella's voice was low and close to her ear. "The one spearheading the rumor mill is Evelyn St. Claire."

"Evelyn?" Sue Ellen watched Stella in the huge mirror in front of her. What in the world was Luke's ex-mother-in-law saying now? Luke was married and the boys had two stable, loving adults to take care of them. There was nothing more she could do about the situation, besides try to get along with everyone. She should be darn thankful that Luke wasn't holding some kind of grudge against her and using the boys as pawns to get his revenge. Luke would never use his sons that way, but she didn't think Evelyn had the same ethics.

"She's been in here a couple of times since your wedding." Stella released some more of the hair from on top of her head.

"So?" She wanted to tell Stella to change the subject, but she couldn't. If Evelyn was spreading rumors about her, then it concerned Luke and the boys. It concerned her marriage.

Stella's whisper grew softer. "She's been hinting at some pretty sordid stuff."

"What sordid stuff?" Sue Ellen had never done anything sordid in her life. She wasn't even sure she would know sordid if she backed into it.

"Evelyn's been wondering, and quite loudly, if I may say so, about your past."

"My past?" She couldn't keep the surprise out of her voice. As far as she knew, she didn't have a past, sordid or otherwise.

"She wants to know why Ron—who, in Evelyn's words, is an upstanding member of this community—called off your engagement a couple of years ago. Evelyn swears something isn't on the up-and-up there. Everyone knows that an engagement is never called off mutually, no matter what both parties say. Evelyn just can't imagine what a sweet, mild-mannered hair dresser like you had done that had been so awful." Stella ran a couple of strands of her hair through her fingers. "The well water out at Luke's place is agreeing with your hair." Stella's voice rose just loud enough for a few to catch her words. "It's softer now."

Sue Ellen stared at her reflection in the mirror and noticed how pale she looked. Evelyn was snooping into business she had no right to be in. It was old business. It had nothing to do with Luke or the boys. Evelyn just wanted to stir up some trouble, any trouble, between herself and Luke. Her husband wouldn't care if she couldn't have any children of her own. He didn't want any more children. He didn't even want to sleep with his wife, so future children were never an issue. Evelyn couldn't harm her or her marriage.

"You okay, Sue Ellen?" The concern in Stella's voice touched her heart. Stella had been a good friend over the years.

She reached up and patted Stella's hand. "I'm fine, Stella. Don't worry about Evelyn. She's just upset that Luke got remarried. It's nothing against me personally. She would be sharpening her claws on anyone who had became Blake and Dalton's stepmom."

"How are the boys doing?" Stella went back to cutting her hair.

The gossip part of her visit was over. Sue Ellen

relaxed and filled her friend in on the joys of motherhood. Her voice was loud enough for the entire shop to hear. When it came to the newness and wonderment of motherhood, she could hold her own against the best. Blake and Dalton were not only the joy of her life, they were her heart. They were her family.

Luke stood in the kitchen and listened to the quiet that surrounded him. Everyone was in bed, including his wife. Sue Ellen had retired within an hour after the boys were asleep. If he was a smart man, he would head upstairs himself. But lately, no one would accuse him of being a smart man. Intelligent men slept with their wives instead of pacing empty rooms and staring at ceilings. A man with only two functioning brain cells would have had enough smarts not to tell a beautiful and desirable woman like Sue Ellen that she was only going to be a wife in name only.

He had been a self-righteous fool, believing he was sacrificing himself on the altar of matrimony for the sake of his sons. He was now dearly paying for that misconception. Sue Ellen was the best thing to ever happen to his sons, or to his own boring life. She had brought springtime into this old farmer's house and he, like the fool he was, was still standing in the bitter coldness of winter.

Luke glanced around the kitchen, and the warmth and the love surrounded him. Sue Ellen had done that to his home and to his sons. Blake and Dalton were basking and growing within that warmth. He hadn't failed his sons.

Tiffany had loved her sons, but it had been a disciplined and proud love. To Tiffany, Blake and Dalton had been objects of affection to hold up and show off. Sue Ellen loved Luke's sons, but it was a softer, warmer love. Sue Ellen was proud to be their mother and there was no need to show them, the house or anything else off to the world.

Sue Ellen seemed content with her role as mother and wife.

Everything had been going so smoothly until the other afternoon, when he had rubbed the kink out of her shoulders and given into the temptation to brush a kiss across the pale, satiny smoothness of her neck. Every male instinct he possessed had told him that Sue Ellen had been just as affected by his touch as he was by touching her. He wanted his wife with a burning need that only intensified with each passing day. What Sue Ellen wanted was a mystery to him. Should he believe the embarrassment and shock that had been clearly expressed on her face, or should he believe the heated hunger that had been burning in the depths of her sky blue eyes?

His experience with women was amazingly limited, considering today's standards. He had married his high-school sweetheart, and she had been his first and only lover. Courting Tiffany had consisted of fast-food meals, drive-in movies and making curfews. He was now walking dangerously on new ground. Very unstable ground.

Something had spooked Sue Ellen. She used to

spend the evenings, after the boys were in bed, in front of the television or reading in the family room. He had begun to look forward to those quiet times. Now his wife tucked the boys into bed, quickly finished up whatever needed to be done and hightailed it up the stairs to her bedroom so fast that he was surprised the carpeting on the steps didn't have scorch marks. Why? Was she afraid he was going to pounce on her, or was she afraid that she might be the one pouncing?

It was an interesting question.

As he walked across the room to turn out the lights, he once again spotted Dalton's pictures plastered on nearly every single inch of the refrigerator. Every crayon drawing contained a dog. A brown furry dog. A black-and-white short-haired mix. A huge black canine that resembled a bear and a brown, long-legged dog that looked more like a horse. Dalton was expressing his wishes with artistic talent. Blake wasn't so diplomatic. Blake came home from school with books on dogs from the library. The boys had been poring over the books, discussing the merits of each and every breed.

When the campaign for a dog had begun, Luke had turned to Sue Ellen for help. His wife seemed to know exactly how to handle his sons. But now she was no help at all. She clearly sided with the boys, and he had caught her glancing through a couple of the dog books. He wasn't sure if Sue Ellen initiated the desire for a puppy, but he knew she wasn't opposed to the idea.

When Blake had been a toddler, he had wanted to

get the boy a puppy. Tiffany had vetoed that idea faster than a jack rabbit with a fox on its scent. Tiffany's reasons had been valid. Since he worked such long hours, she would have been the one to take care of the dog, clean up the accidents, feed it, vacuum up all the hair and do anything else an active puppy would require. Besides, Tiffany had point-blank refused to allow an animal into her house. The subject of puppies, kittens or even goldfish never arose again.

Until now.

He reached over, turned off the lights and quietly walked out of the room and up the stairs. He stood in the hallway and glanced into each of the boys' rooms to make sure they were covered. Blake had a habit of kicking off his blankets and freezing the rest of the night. Tonight Blake was still covered. Luke turned away from the sight of his sleeping son and continued down the hall.

A pale strip of light was coming from beneath Sue Ellen's door. His feet halted at her door. His wife was still awake. Probably reading one of the blood-and-guts murder mysteries she seemed so fond of. How could such a gently loving soul love to read about mayhem and madness? He wondered what she would do if he opened the door and crawled in between her yellow gingham sheets with her. Would she welcome him with open arms or scream the house down? Interesting questions. Questions he wasn't about to find the answers to tonight, no matter how much he ached.

With a muttered curse he pulled the tattered remnants of his control together and continued down the hall. He opened the door to the master bedroom and flipped on the light. Bright lights illuminated the room. He closed his eyes for a moment before glancing wishfully over his shoulder at Sue Ellen's closed door. He shook his head at things that couldn't be, at least for now. He turned, glanced at his own bedroom and muttered, "Lord, I hate pink."

Evelyn St. Claire stood in the kitchen with a scowl on her face. "It didn't take you long, did it?"

Sue Ellen's fingers trembled slightly as she neatly wrapped the loaf of banana nut bread in aluminum foil. She knew exactly what Evelyn was referring to—the change in the kitchen—but she decided to play dumb. Sometimes stupidity had its reward. "Long for what?" she asked pleasantly.

"You might be able to change wallpaper, but you won't be able to erase the memory of my daughter."

"I'm not trying to erase Tiffany's memory." Luke was upstairs with the boys, making sure they had packed everything they would need for an overnight stay at their grandparents'. She wished Luke would hurry. Evelyn wasn't dealing with the changes very well. "Blake told me that his grandpop loves banana nut bread, so I baked Frank a loaf." She handed Evelyn the still-warm foil-wrapped loaf. "He wasn't sure what kind of bread you might like."

Evelyn placed the bread on the kitchen table next to her purse. "I never realized you were so domesticated."

Sue Ellen gritted her teeth and managed to pull

off a small smile. "Neither did I. Blake and Dalton are such a joy to take care of, they make everything seem so easy." Evelyn was making this harder than it needed to be, but that seemed to be Evelyn's way.

When Blake and Dalton's grandmother had called Wednesday night, Sue Ellen had been the one to answer the phone. The conversation she had had with Stella in the beauty shop was still playing heavily on her mind. She didn't want Evelyn as an enemy, but she wasn't foolish enough to think they could actually be friends. She would settle for polite tolerance, for the sake of the boys.

In a way she understood Evelyn's pain. The woman had lost her daughter, her only child. The grief and pain must still be unbearable, even though it had happened nearly two years earlier. Evelyn had been playing an active part in the boys' life, but that had diminished greatly when Luke and she had gotten married.

It had been Sue Ellen's idea that the boys might enjoy a sleep-over. Evelyn had pounced on the suggestion, and the date had been set for Friday night. Luke had agreed to the plan. Now, facing a hostile Evelyn across the kitchen, Sue Ellen wasn't so sure this was a good idea.

"Here we are, all packed and ready." Luke followed the boys into the room. Each carried his own duffle bag. Both bags looked big enough to contain a week's worth of clothes.

Sue Ellen smiled as both boys ran across the room and threw their arms around Evelyn, shouting, "Grandmom, we're ready."

"Can we have pizza?" asked Dalton.

"Can we rent movies?" asked Blake.

Evelyn's tender smile for her grandsons made Sue Ellen feel as if she had made the right decision after all. "Yes and yes." Evelyn hugged both boys. "You can have anything you want."

Luke rolled his eyes toward the ceiling, and Sue Ellen had to suppress a groan of dismay. Pizza and movies were fine; it was the other part of that statement that gave her pause. Evelyn didn't seem to be in the mood tonight to talk over some ground rules. She took a deep breath and refused to lose what was left of her tattered smile. One night of being totally spoiled wouldn't harm the boys.

"Let's go, boys. Grandpop's at home warming up the VCR." Evelyn picked up her purse and opened the door.

Blake ran to his father and gave him a hug. 'Bye, Dad." Then he ran to her, hugged her and placed a kiss on her cheek. " 'Bye, Sue Ellen."

" 'Bye." She knelt down and ruffled Blake's hair. "You behave and listen to your grandmother."

Dalton hugged and kissed his father before throwing his arms around her neck and giving her a half dozen noisy kisses. " 'Bye, Mom."

She kissed him back, ruffled his hair and said, " 'Bye, Dalt. Mind your grandmother."

Sue Ellen was standing back up when she noticed the look of pure fury on Evelyn's face. What in the world . . . ? Both boys ran past their grandmother and out the door without noticing that the woman had gone first deathly pale and then raging red. By the curse Luke just muttered, he'd obviously noticed Evelyn's expression.

It took Sue Ellen two heartbeats to realize what had just happened. Dalton had called her "Mom." By the look on Evelyn's face, she was going to put a stop to that immediately. She felt her heart sink as Evelyn opened her mouth.

Before one word emerged, Luke grabbed Evelyn's elbow and hustled her out the front door. Luke gave her a quick look and said, "I'll be right back." The door closed behind them.

Sue Ellen stood in the silence of the house and swore she could actually feel her heart breaking in two. In the distance she heard Luke yell for the boys to get into the car, that Grandmom would be right there. She turned from the door and stared at the warm loaf of banana nut bread still sitting on the kitchen table. Evelyn had forgotten it. More likely she'd purposely left it behind. The only thing Evelyn wanted from her was for her to go away.

She wasn't going to accommodate her.

Through the door the sounds of voices being raised in an argument could be heard, but not the words. Luke was defending her. His relationship with Evelyn was rocky to start with, and now he was exacerbating it more because of her.

She didn't think she could possibly feel any worse. Tears filled her eyes as she carried the bread over to the counter, placed it there and then walked out of the room.

She was standing in the family room, looking out the window at the fields, when she heard a car start up and drive away. The front door opened, then closed. A moment later Luke stepped into the room, but she didn't turn around to look at him. She didn't want him to see her tears. "Sorry."

"You have nothing to be sorry for, Sue Ellen." Luke came up behind her, but didn't touch her. "Dalton is the one who wants to call you 'Mom.' It wasn't the other way around, even though I know you love it when he calls you that."

"Dalton's going to get a lecture from his grandmother about respecting his mother's memory. He's too young to understand any of this. He's going to think he's doing something wrong." The tears had overflowed and she quickly swiped at them. She was being silly. What did it matter if Dalton called her mom or not? Blake didn't call her mom, and she loved him just as much as she loved Dalton.

Luke gently turned her around to face him. "You're wrong about that. Dalton understands enough to know what a mother is, and to him, you are his mother." Luke's fingers brushed away another tear. "Evelyn won't say a word to him about calling you 'Mom.' "

"Why won't she? You saw her expression, Luke. She was furious."

"Because I told her that if she did, or if she got either of the boys upset tonight, she wouldn't get to see them, let alone have them spend nights at her place."

"You told her that?" Lord, Evelyn must have blown a gasket the size of Detroit at that bit of news. Why was Luke being so darn nice to her?

WIFE IN NAME ONLY 135

"I've never seen Blake or Dalton so happy and contented as in the past couple of weeks. You did that, Sue Ellen. Not me, not Evelyn, but you. I'll not have Evelyn making mischief and ruining everything." Luke took a step closer and gently wiped at the last tear rolling down her cheek.

She blinked away the moisture pooling in her eyes. Tears never solved anything. "You're a wonderful father, Luke. It's you who makes the boys so happy and contented, not me." She didn't deserve the credit for Blake's and Dalton's happiness. Luke did.

Luke shook his head and lowered his gaze to her mouth. "You're wrong. It's you who is so wonderful." The rough pad of his thumb traced her lower lip.

She managed a small watery smile. "We're both a wonder."

"Yeah." Luke's voice was barely a whisper. A hot, velvety whisper. "You're not going to cry anymore, are you?"

She shook her head and whispered against his thumb, "No, why?" Her heart was slamming against her chest and she was getting a really strange, warm feeling in the pit of her stomach.

"Seeing you cry makes me want to do crazy things." Luke's rich brown eyes darkened to near black as he continued to gaze at her mouth.

"What kind of crazy things?" Her gaze was locked on his mouth. Lord, how she wanted his mouth.

"Like kissing you."

She felt her heart slam against her breast. "You want to kiss me when I'm crying?"

"No." Luke shook his head as his thumb stroked her mouth. "I want to kiss you all the time."

"You do?" She arched her body closer to his heat. The tips of her breasts lightly brushed against the material of his shirt. She nearly sighed.

"Oh, yeah." Luke's arms slowly went around her and pulled her closer. "What would you do if I kissed you right now?"

She couldn't even contemplate lying to him. She had been waiting for this moment her entire life. Her gaze locked with his and she gave him the truth. "I'd melt."

"Oh, Sue Ellen"—Luke took a shuddered breath and arched his hips against hers—"you shouldn't have told me that."

Before she could think of a response, Luke lowered his head and captured her mouth.

SEVEN

Luke couldn't resist the temptation for one minute more. He had to discover what Sue Ellen tasted like or he would go out of his mind. The polite, formal kiss he had given her at the church on their wedding day had been more brotherly than husbandly. He had seen his sons kiss Sue Ellen with more passion.

His mouth covered hers, and he sank into the temptation. Sweet fire burned his mouth and ignited his soul. His arms wrapped around Sue Ellen's slender body and pulled her closer. He deepened the kiss and relished the passion. Savored the heat.

Sue Ellen had been wrong. She wasn't the one melting, he was. He was melting on the inside and hardening on the outside. His body was turning into rock, while his heart was jackhammering hard enough to crack granite. Hot blood pumped through his veins and liquid fire melted his gut. Every ounce of melted fire pooled behind the zipper of his jeans. He was fully aroused and throbbing before his tongue even swept past Sue Ellen's lips.

He had to taste all of her.

A sound of startled passion emerged from the back of Sue Ellen's throat. That enticing sound went directly to his head and to his groin. His wife was just as aroused as he was. He deepened the kiss and pulled her closer. The heavenly weight of her breasts pressed into his chest and the urgent demand of her hips rocked against his arousal.

A groan of pure heat escaped his throat before he could stop it. Sue Ellen captured his groan and nipped at his lower lip. Desire pulled at his gut and shattered his control. He slid his hands down her back and cupped her sweetly curved bottom. She fit perfectly in his hands. His mouth released Sue Ellen's lips and blazed a trail of moist kisses down her throat as he lifted her and pressed his straining arousal to the juncture of her thighs. Slim yet strong legs encircled his hips. Sue Ellen's smooth throat arched beneath his lips, giving him greater access as he slid his mouth lower. Their ragged breathing filled the room.

He lifted his mouth from the wildly pounding pulse in Sue Ellen's throat. His gaze lowered to the perfectly rounded breasts straining against the white cotton of her T-shirt. Twin berry-sized nipples were crowning each enticing globe. All he had to do was lift her slightly higher and he could press a kiss on each one of those protruding nubs.

He gazed up and away from the temptation. Sue Ellen's eyes were opened and glazed as she sucked in another lungful of air. Her beautiful clear blue eyes were now dark and turbulent, like a storm-tossed sea. He could read the desire and need in their depths. Her lips were moist and slightly swollen from his kisses. His breathing was harsh and uneven, and he had to swallow twice before he could manage to get a word past his constricted throat. "If you're going to stop this, it has to be now."

Sue Ellen gazed at Luke and wondered if he had suddenly lost his mind. He thought she would actually call a halt to this heat? Fire was consuming her body faster than it would have devoured the savanna in Africa. It hadn't started at her toes and worked its way up; the molten fire had started at the center of her being and had been ignited the instant Luke's mouth settled on hers.

Her breasts were swollen and pouting for his attention and she could feel the hard column of his arousal pressing against her thighs. She was breathing so fast and shaky that she doubted she would be able to string two words together. She shook her head in response to his question.

"No what?" Luke left a trail of moist hot kisses to the corner of her mouth. "No, you want to stop, or no, you don't want to stop?"

She turned her head and slid her tongue provocatively over his lower lip. She grinned when she felt the shudder that racked his body. Luke wanted her, as much as she wanted him. "You stop now, I'll burn your cornfields."

Her fingers slipped into his hair. The short brown strands felt like silk, just like she knew they would. She had been fantasizing about running her fingers through his hair for weeks now. The rough stubble covering his jaw spoke of an early morning shave. She pressed her mouth against the bristle and ran her tongue lightly up Luke's jaw to tenderly bite his earlobe when he chuckled. The sound was deep and rusty, as if he wasn't used to laughing playfully. She melted more.

"I'd do just about anything to save that crop." Luke's teeth pulled gently at her lower lip as he arched his hips, pressing himself more fully against her.

She tightened her legs and prayed Luke wouldn't put her down. She would never be able to stand. She didn't even recognize her own voice when she whispered against his hot and hungry lips, "Anything?"

Anything covered a lot of territory, and she wanted to experience it all with Luke. Only with Luke. He was making her feel things she never thought she would feel. Desire, hot and thick, pulsed through her body, making her feel empty. An emptiness that only Luke could fill.

Luke's mouth barely lifted. "How important is a bed to you?"

She pulled his head back down and kissed him with all the heat she was feeling. When he lifted his mouth again, she grabbed a quick breath. "The only thing I need is you, Luke." Strong fingers grasped her bottom and pulled her closer to his straining arousal. The only thing separating them was denim. Too many clothes. She needed to feel the heat of his skin beneath her fingers and his thickness as he filled the void inside her trembling body.

With fingers that quivered with anticipation, she started to unbutton Luke's shirt. Brown curls teased her fingers and heat warmed her hands. The rapid pounding of Luke's heart beneath her hands sent a jolt of pleasure through her. She bent and placed a light kiss directly above the hammering.

Luke hissed and glanced across the room. "The couch is too far."

Early evening sunshine bathed his chest as she tugged the shirttails out of his jeans and tried to push the offending article off his shoulders. It wouldn't go, because he wasn't releasing her bottom. Her lips teased the darkened nub poking its way out of the dark curls covering his chest. Her tongue circled the darkened disk. She felt the shudder that shook his body and smiled. "Who needs a couch?"

Before she could grab her next breath, she was flat on her back on the carpet. Luke's long, hard body was positioned over her, but he wasn't touching her. His arms were supporting his body and he was gazing down at her with such an intense look that she was beginning to worry that he would leave. She reached up and gently cupped his cheek. "What's wrong?"

Luke slowly shook his head. "Nothing's wrong." He turned his head and kissed the center of her palm. "I was just thinking how beautiful you are."

She shook her head and smiled. Luke thought she was beautiful. It was a nice thought, but it wasn't true. She knew what she looked like. Her eyes were a clear sky blue and she considered them her best feature. Her mouth was too generous and her nose tilted up ever so slightly at its end, giving her a "perky" look. It had been okay at sixteen, but at twenty-seven she didn't want to be called perky. The dusting of freckles that appeared each spring and faded by Christmas only added to the childish impression. Luke didn't need to whisper sweet compliments into her ear to get her into his bed. She was more than willing. "Passable, maybe, but not beautiful."

Luke bent his head and kissed her so lightly, it felt like the brush of a butterfly's wing against her lips. "I'll show you how beautiful you are." When his mouth returned, it was hot and hungry.

She wrapped her arms around his shoulders and pulled him down on top of her as she matched him kiss for kiss. Tongues mated and teeth nipped as she worked his shirt off his shoulders and ran her hands up and down his muscular back.

Luke broke the kiss and yanked her shirt up and over her head. His mouth was liquid heat as it outlined the lacy edges of her bra.

She threaded her fingers into his hair and pressed herself more fully against his mouth. She needed Luke's mouth on her, all of her. Warm lips closed over one of the peaks of her breasts and she arched her hips and rubbed against the thick column of his arousal. Liquid heat rushed to the juncture of her thighs. Her trembling fingers reached for his belt buckle. "Too many clothes."

Luke's tongue circled her belly button as her bra was unhooked and tossed to the side. "I agree."

Her fingers were quivering so much, she fumbled with the buckle and couldn't get it undone. Luke's hands gently brushed hers away as he rolled to the side and took over the task for her. She watched enthralled as denim jeans and cotton boxers were pushed down over his narrow hips and long legs.

Luke yanked off his socks, leaving himself totally naked before turning back to her.

Luke stopped before taking her back into his arms. He was stretched out beside her, bathed in golden sunlight. She let her gaze travel from the tip of his toes up to the burning darkness of his brown eyes. Luke's eyes held a thousand questions, and just a hint of anxiety. It was that small show of insecurity that had her relaxing and not panicky. She swallowed hard. "Impressive." She was more than impressed, she was leaning more to the apprehensive side. She wasn't a virgin, but her few previous experiences hadn't been so well-endowed.

Luke's smile was slow in coming, but it was more powerful because of it. She felt that smile down to her toes. It was Luke's first smile that didn't have a thing to do with the boys. This smile was just for her.

Luke's smile slowly faded as he reached out a hand, and with the tip of one finger gently circled one of her nipples. She watched the lean, tan finger lightly brush across the hardened nub. She sucked in a harsh breath.

Luke glanced up and smiled once again. "Like I said, beautiful." Work-callused fingers skimmed her abdomen and unsnapped her jeans.

She could hear the grate of each tooth as her zipper was lowered. Luke's breath caressed her stomach as she arched her hips and felt the denim of her jeans being brushed over her thighs and down her legs. The triangle of black silk slowly followed. A soft kiss caressed the inside of her ankle.

Her heart beat faster as Luke's mouth traveled up

her calf and brushed her knee. Hot fingers stroked the inside of her thighs as her legs parted. She forgot how to breathe. She forgot how to think. All she could do was feel. Lord, how she felt each stroke of his tongue and lips, each caress of his fingers and the warm, rough texture of his palms as they slid up the sensitive skin of her inner thighs, spreading them farther.

Strong yet gentle fingers wove their way through the nest of curls capping the moist center of her being. The center that was yearning to be filled. She arched her hips and felt Luke slide a finger deep inside her. The desire spiraled higher.

A moan of pleasure was torn from her throat as one finger became two and the ache burning inside her became a mountain of raw need. She was at the peak and she wanted Luke with her when she went over the edge. Her arms reached for him and his name was whispered in a plea. "Luke."

A husky whisper was muttered against her thigh, but he didn't move up her body. He did something worse, much worse. His mouth replaced his finger and she nearly went over the edge without him. She shuddered and tried to grab his shoulders but couldn't reach him.

Luke must have sensed how close she was to the edge, because he stopped the blissful torture and strung kisses up her quivering belly, across her aching breasts and nipped at her jaw. She wrapped her legs around his hips and captured his mouth as he slowly started to fill the void. Desire rippled through her, and she deepened the kiss. Luke slowly started to stroke and she realized the peak of ecstasy was still ahead of her.

With every thrust she climbed higher. Her arms pulled Luke closer and she stroked his damp back and urgently grasped his buttocks. Their tongues were a moist mating, matching them thrust for thrust. Breathing seemed inconsequential. The only thing that mattered was finding the promised release.

She had never been this high, never felt the thousand and one nerve endings screaming throughout her body. Everything was converging into one gigantic pressure cooker, and the lid was about to go exploding off. She squeezed her thighs and clung tighter to Luke. He increased the pace. The impending explosion would have been frightening, if it wasn't so pleasurable. She hurried to her fate and allowed Luke to lead. If she hung on to him, she would be okay. Luke would never harm her. He would keep her safe.

Luke bit her lip and muttered something halfway between a curse and a prayer. He was wild. She was wild, and the edge was directly in front of her. She couldn't go any higher. Luke thrust one more time and she went spiraling off the mountaintops crying his name.

In the distance she heard Luke shout her name. His body shook and trembled with his release. Or maybe it was her release shaking him. She couldn't tell where he ended and where she started. It really didn't matter.

***

Luke lay in the fading sunlight, cradling Sue Ellen's warm naked body and wondering if he would ever get his breathing back to normal. Nothing would be normal ever again. What in the hell had just happened?

He knew the basics of lovemaking and considered himself pretty well experienced even though he had had only one other lover in his life. He had been married for seven years, after all. But it had never felt like this. Nothing had ever felt like this

His arms tightened around Sue Ellen as her rapid breathing caressed his chest. He felt a little bit better, knowing that she was experiencing the same difficulties trying to catch her breath. His chest cushioned her head and her long, silky, golden hair was tangled across his arm. One wayward strand was tickling his nose. He reached up and brushed at the silken web. He took a deep, steadying breath and asked, "Are you all right?" Lord knew he wasn't.

Sue Ellen mumbled something against his chest. Her lips had moved, but not one other body part. He couldn't help it; he chuckled. He had never had quite this effect on any other woman. His laughter slowly faded. Then again, no woman had ever had this effect on him.

"Is that a yes or a no?" His hand slowly stroked the womanly flare of her hip. Desire that had been hot and heavy moments before was warm and pulsing now. He liked having Sue Ellen pressed against him, all warm and satisfied. The only thing missing was a nice soft bed beneath them. The thick carpet in the family room was nice to walk on, but he didn't think

WIFE IN NAME ONLY 147

DuPont had this activity in mind when they wear-tested the fibers.

"It's a yes, but don't ask me to move." A quick kiss landed on his stomach.

He felt his stomach muscles clench and his breath hitch in his throat. The slow, steady pulse of desire arced into something wild and unpredictable. He wanted Sue Ellen again, but he'd be damned if he would take her on the floor again, like some hormone-driven teenager. Hell, he had never been this horny as a teenager. Not five minutes ago he had spent every ounce of energy he had possessed. By the stirring in his loins and by Sue Ellen's quick intake of breath, he would have to say he was about to get his second wind.

With a silent prayer that not all his strength had been spent, he rolled away from Sue Ellen and stood up.

Sue Ellen's sleepy blue eyes widened slightly as they gazed up at him. "Where are you going?"

He bent down and picked her up into his arms and headed out of the room. He stumbled slightly when one of his feet got tangled in her bra, but his legs held out as he carried her up the stairs. "I need a shower." He had been working outside all day and had only come in to help the boys pack for their overnight visit with their grandparents. If he had known what was going to happen once the boys were out of the house, he would have come in earlier and showered beforehand. As it was, he was determined to shower before he got his tempting little wife into a bed. Hell, the way he was feeling, they wouldn't be getting out of bed anytime soon.

Gentle arms circled his neck and a teasing nip tugged at his ear. "I seem to be a little bit sweaty myself."

He pulled her closer to his chest and felt the sweet curve of her bottom brush against his arousal with every step he took. He rolled his eyes heavenward and prayed for strength. "Behave, or we're not going to make it far." If she bit his ear one more time, he was taking her in the hallway, and the hell with soft beds and cotton sheets.

He pushed open the door to the main bath and carefully reached into the tub to start the water. He could have taken Sue Ellen to the master bathroom and used the shower in there, but somehow this room seemed more appropriate. At one end of the tub was Sue Ellen's shampoo and flowery-scented body wash. At the other end was his sons' shampoo and a fleet of plastic boats.

Before Sue Ellen could protest, he stepped into the tub, with her still in his arms. Sue Ellen shrieked a protest as the water poured over them. The water was cool, but it was quickly warming. Sue Ellen squirmed, and he nearly dropped her. Wet bodies meant slick bodies.

He slowly lowered her to her feet and brushed a quick kiss across her swollen mouth. "Can you stand?"

Sue Ellen swept a wet lock of hair away from her face. "Sure."

He would have to have been blind not to notice the flush sweeping up her cheeks. The cool water slicing over his body had had the desired affect on his hot and throbbing arousal. They just might make it to that bed after all. He adjusted the water to a warmer level. "What's wrong?"

"I, um..."—Sue Ellen looked flustered for a moment—"never showered with anyone before."

"It's easy." He picked up the nylon puff and squirted some of her flowery soap on it. "I'll wash your back, you wash mine." He turned her slightly and gently started to wash every square inch of her incredible body. The red brush marks on the pale rounded curve of her bottom caused him to berate himself for his impatience. He knelt and kissed each irritated cheek. "Next time, I'll take the bottom." As the fragrant suds drifted down her legs, his mouth caressed the slick wet skin.

He worked the puff up the front of her body. He felt the shivers of desire that racked her body but didn't stop his leisurely tour of warm suds and gentle kisses. By the time he had worked his way back to her shoulders he was hard as iron and breathing heavily. Sue Ellen's blue eyes looked hot and hungry. Her mouth was parted, silently waiting for him. Silently begging him to take it. He pulled her into his arms and kissed her with an answering hunger of his own. When he couldn't take another minute of it, he broke the kiss and reached for the faucet. "We're out of here before I try something really stupid." Making love in the shower was either an act of stupidity or suicide. He wasn't about to risk Sue Ellen's delicious body.

A warm trembling hand closed over his before he could turn off the faucet. "My turn to wash your back." She picked up the puff he had dropped when he had kissed her.

He desperately shook his head. He would never be able to withstand the torture without taking her and risking both their lives or limbs. He nodded at the puff. "It smells like flowers."

A warm smile curved her mouth as she rinsed out the netting and applied whatever his sons used. A slender finger told him to turn around and face the wall. He complied only because he didn't want Sue Ellen to think he couldn't stand up to the same torture he had just put her through.

A tender rubbing caressed his back, his buttocks and his legs. He closed his eyes and clenched his teeth as soft hands stroked every inch available.

"Turn around." Sue Ellen was kneeling at his feet. Her generous mouth was inches away from his thighs.

He silently groaned, half a curse, half a prayer, but he turned. Her tender fingers worked their way up his calves and over his knees. His breath hitched higher as she worked suds into his thighs. His eyes flew open as the suds and her fingers worked their way into the thatch of curls at the base of his manhood. He jerked back and nearly lost his balance.

Sue Ellen's hands stroked the length of his arousal, and his breath hissed as water pummeled his back. Nothing was as sweet and hot as Sue Ellen's fingers wrapped around him. Downstairs, earlier, she hadn't touched him. He hadn't given her the chance, knowing that he could never have controlled himself if she had. He closed his eyes and arched his hips as every fantasy, every dream from the past few weeks came flooding back with just a touch.

He nearly lost it when a soft kiss landed on his thigh. A harsh groan filled the shower as he lifted Sue Ellen to her feet.

"Luke?" Confusion and desire clouded Sue Ellen's beautiful face.

"Too dangerous." He took the netting from her fingers and with a few brisk strokes finished washing his chest and arms. He quickly rinsed, and then with an impatient gesture twisted off the water and pushed back the curtain.

Within minutes he had Sue Ellen dried and her long hair wrapped in a towel. His own body was half-heartedly dried as he pulled his wife out into the hallway. The master bedroom with its queen-size bed was at the end of the hall. With the same feeling of rightness that he had chosen the bathroom, he pulled Sue Ellen into her bedroom. He wasn't sure who pulled who down onto the bed, but it didn't matter. Before the towel unraveled from her hair, he was deep inside her and they were both rushing toward the inevitable.

The small contractions of Sue Ellen's climax pulled him over the edge and he shouted her name as the world shifted beneath him for the second time in one night.

Five minutes later he stared at the white lace curtains on the window and marveled at the darkness beyond. It was after eight o'clock and they hadn't had dinner yet. His stomach was rumbling, but he was too content and satisfied to leave Sue Ellen's bed.

Making love in a bed definitely had some advantages over the floor. Soft pillows and a warm blanket to cover rapidly cooling bodies were just a few. Hearing the sigh of pleasure Sue Ellen had breathed as she snuggled closer to him was another. Knowing that her adorable little tush wasn't going to suffer any more rug burns was another.

He pressed a kiss to the top of her head. "Okay?"

A nod was his only answer. He tightened his hold and wrinkled his nose. What was that smell? He could pick out the floral scent of Sue Ellen's soap and the herbal scent of her shampoo. The lemony scent of the fabric softener used on the sheets was the same as his sheets, and even the musky essence of their lovemaking he could detect. But what was that other odor? He had been smelling it since the shower.

With a sense of dread he lifted his arm and took a whiff of his forearm. "Sue Ellen?"

"Yes." A baby-fine cheek rubbed against the curls on his chest.

"What kind of soap did you use on me?" He already knew the answer, but he wanted to hear her say it.

"I used the boys', since I knew you wouldn't want to smell like a florist shop." A kiss landed directly above his heart.

He could hear the laughter in her voice. She was going to pay for this, even though he was just as much to blame as she was. He had been standing right there when she applied the liquid soap to the netting. If his gaze could have left her pebble-hard nipples or his mind got higher than his waist, he would have realized there was only one other kind of soap to use. "You think this is funny, don't you?"

Sue Ellen giggled. "No, I think it's sexy."

"You think a grown man smelling like bubble gum is sexy?" Now that he had identified the smell it was nearly overwhelming.

Sue Ellen lifted her head and grinned at him. "I think it smells delicious." She slowly licked her lips in anticipation. "In fact, I think it smells so delicious that I just have to find out how it tastes."

A moan of pure pleasure vibrated in the back of his throat as her tongue slowly stroked his chest. He was buying a case of that soap. Just as soon as he could manage to force himself to get out of his wife's bed.

It was nearly ten o'clock before they made it downstairs to the kitchen. Sue Ellen tightened the sash of her faded yellow robe and turned the bacon sizzling in the pan. She glanced over at Luke as he set the table and poured the orange juice. Both of them were hungry but neither had wanted to make a big production out of dinner, so they had settled on bacon and eggs. A quick and easy meal. She returned her gaze to the frying pan. There had been nothing quick about the way Luke had made love to her that last time. He had been so darn thorough and slow, she had actually been begging for her release before he was done pleasuring her. And pleasure her, he did.

"Is it almost ready?" asked Luke as he expertly buttered two more pieces of toast. The intimate smile he gave her nearly melted her knees.

Three times! The man had made love to her three times, and all three times she had climaxed and shattered within his arms. It was amazing, truly phenomenal. She didn't think men could do it three times in one evening. Weren't they the ones who were always whining about needing time to regain their energy? Luke obviously had an abundance of energy. Hell, the man could power a nuclear power plant.

"Sue Ellen?" Luke's voice penetrated her musing.

"What?" The bacon was burning, and she quickly removed it from the pan. The eggs looked perfect as she slid them onto their plates.

"I asked if it was almost done." Luke shook his head and took the two plates from her hands.

"I'm sorry. My mind must have been drifting." *Boy, had it been drifting . . . straight back to her bed with its rumpled sheets.* She willed the blush sweeping up her cheeks to go away. From Luke's amused expression, she had a feeling she hadn't succeeded.

"Penny for your thoughts?" Luke placed the plates on the table and held out her chair.

She shook her head and quickly sat down. Luke's fingers were warm and gentle as they brushed aside her hair. He placed a kiss on the back of her neck. "How about a dime?"

She glanced over her shoulder at him and noticed that his gaze was on the deep *V* of her chenille robe, where a wanton display of cleavage showed. Her blush intensified. Neither of them had a stitch of clothing on beneath their robes. Her fingers trembled as she clutched the lapels of her robe tighter together. Luke had seen, kissed and tasted every square inch of her body, yet the heat of his gaze could still make her blush.

Luke's lips brushed the side of her throat. "I would pay dearly to know exactly where that blush starts."

She had no idea where it started, but she wasn't about to open the front of her robe to find out. The fiery flush seemed to encompass her entire body. From the tips of her toes to the roots of her hair. She felt a jolt of awareness as Luke's lips nuzzled the pulse at the side of her neck. How was it possible to want this man again after what they had just shared?

She pushed thoughts of tumbling back into bed with Luke to the back of her mind. They had to eat their dinner to replenish their strength. She pulled the lapels of her robe tighter and higher and tried to look mysterious. "A woman needs to have some secrets, Luke."

Before Luke could comment on that statement, his stomach rumbled, and she chuckled. "Eat your dinner before it gets cold."

"Yes, ma'am." Luke pulled out his chair and sat down next to her. He started to eat like a lumberjack deprived of food for a week, but he watched her every move as he took each bite.

She self-consciously picked at the food on her own plate. Usually Luke sat at one end of the table and she at the other. Blake and Dalton filled the middle with their laughter and their stories. Their sons demanded and received all their attention. Now, with them at their grandparents, there was nothing to divert their attention. She nervously played with her fork and noticed the paper napkin Luke had folded precisely in half that had been tucked beneath it. Luke had never helped her with dinner before, leaving the kitchen entirely her domain, but he appeared to be domesticated. She had to wonder if Tiffany had trained him, or had he acquired the skills after his first wife's death

She didn't want to think about Tiffany and what Luke's life had been like with her. That was in his past. She was more concerned about their future together. When Luke asked her to become his wife, it was to be in name only. The rules had changed. Luke had been the one to initiate the change by kissing her in the family room earlier, but she had wholeheartedly gone along with it. So where did they stand now? Was this a once or, more accurately, a three and done deal, or was her husband planning to share her bed every night—or just when the mood struck him?

She stared down at the three strips of bacon on her plate and felt her stomach rebel. Things had moved too fast and she now had no idea where she stood with Luke or within the confines of their marriage. She slowly placed her fork back onto her plate.

"What's wrong?" Luke was staring at her.

The concern in his eyes pulled at her heart, but she couldn't tell Luke the truth. She glanced at the empty seats at the table. "I was just wondering how Blake and Dalton are making out."

"They're fine. For all their bluster and high-handedness, Frank and Evelyn love those boys. They won't let anything happen to them." Luke dug back into his eggs, but he continued to study her. He washed down his meal with a glass of orange juice. "Tell me something, Sue Ellen."

"What?" She picked at a slice of toast.

"Do you miss being a hairdresser?" Luke grabbed a slice himself.

"No." She shook her head. "I thought I would, but I honestly don't."

"What about living in town? Do you miss living in the center of it all, being surrounded by people and having your parents living just a couple of streets over?"

"Wild Rose isn't a thriving city, Luke. They still roll up the sidewalks by nine o'clock. There isn't that much difference living out here. It's quieter, but I like the silence."

"What about your parents?" Luke's gaze was intense and probing.

"What about them? They're only a fifteen-minute drive away. It's not like I moved to New York or California, for cripes' sake." What in the world was Luke getting at? Why this sudden need to know how she was adjusting to living on a farm? "Why the questions?"

"No reason." Luke's gaze left her face and shot over to the clock on the wall. "If you're not too tired, there's a really good movie coming on in about ten minutes." Luke stood up and started to clean off the table.

She frowned at the piece of half-eaten toast in her hand. Luke wasn't telling her the truth. There had been a reason for all his curious questions, but he didn't want to tell her. Why? Didn't he trust her with the truth, or was he so sure she wouldn't like the reason behind the questions? Neither was a pleasant choice.

She pushed back her chair, dropped the toast onto her still full plate and stood. There was no sense borrowing trouble. It would come soon enough. She managed a small smile as she faced the man who had just turned her entire life around with one passion-filled evening. "A movie sounds great."

EIGHT

The sound of a truck driving up the driveway and Dalton's shouts were Sue Ellen's first hint that Luke was back from his mysterious outing. Blake's cries that "Dad's home" confirmed it. She stood up and brushed off the dirt coating the knees of her jeans. Since Luke had left two hours ago she had been in her vegetable garden, weeding and nurturing the plants along. The boys had split their time between the tree house and bugging her to tell them where Luke had gone. She couldn't tell them because she honestly hadn't a clue as to where he had been going.

Luke's hints of his mysterious outing had started Wednesday night and had continued until he got into his pickup early Saturday morning. Whatever Luke was up to must be pretty important. Her husband had seemed awfully proud of himself.

Sue Ellen left the fence-enclosed garden and headed for the now parked pickup truck. Her heart slammed against her ribs and actually picked up a beat or two at the sight of Luke stepping out of the cab. They had been lovers for a couple of weeks and still the mere sight of his long, lean body caused her breath to hitch in the back of her throat. She knew every inch of that body by sight, feel and taste, and it still had the power to move her. Lord, he was gorgeous. She stopped to enjoy the view.

Blake and Dalton came running across the driveway, straight for their dad. "Dad, where did you go?" asked Blake.

"What did you get?" shouted Dalton.

Luke smiled and greeted his sons and then looked at her. A wide grin, just for her, spread across his tan face. That grin went directly to her heart. "Come on, Sue Ellen, you're in on this, too."

She didn't know if she liked the sound of that or not. From the ominous tone of his voice she didn't know whether she was going to enjoy his surprise or not. She slowly started walking again. Over Blake's and Dalton's questions and Luke's low murmurs she heard another sound.

Blake and Dalton heard the sound at the exact same moment. Both boys froze in midquestion and then slowly turned toward the pickup truck.

The passenger-side window was rolled up, but the sound grew louder as two tiny paws and a head appeared. The puppy took one look at the boys and started to yelp wildly. She wouldn't have labeled it quite a bark. It was more of a high-pitched whinny

"A dog!" Blake ran for the truck with Dalton right on his heels.

Dalton's voice echoed across the cornfields. "Puppy, puppy, puppy!"

"Stop, Blake. Don't open that door." Luke hurried to the truck. "Ozzie will fall out."

"Ozzie?" Blake and Dalton pressed their faces up against the window and stared at the puppy. Ozzie was trying desperately to bark, lick or paw his way through the glass.

"Is his name Ozzie, dad?" Dalton's nose was pressed so hard against the glass, Sue Ellen was beginning to fear it would be permanently damaged.

Luke opened the driver's door and the puppy disappeared from sight. A moment later Luke walked around the back of the truck carrying a squirming bundle of brown-and-white fur. He placed the excited puppy on the ground. Ozzie obviously didn't know who to run to first. He danced around in circles, stepping on feet and pawing at knees. Blake and Dalton danced right along with him. Hands, paws and a long, pink puppy tongue were everywhere. Blake and Dalton couldn't seem to stop grinning or laughing.

Luke walked over to her and smiled. She smiled back and then turned her attention back to the boys and the puppy. "Who named him Ozzie?" Lord, the puppy was adorable, and she couldn't remember ever seeing the boys so excited.

"I did. The way the boys seem to take such joy in disagreeing with each other, I figured they would never come up with a name they would both agree upon." Luke moved up behind her, wrapped his arms around her waist and plopped his chin on her shoulder. His gaze seemed to be centered on the boys.

She stiffened for a moment, but then relaxed into

his warmth. Luke very rarely showed any signs of affection toward her in front of the boys. Of course they were so busy with the puppy, Luke could probably drag her into the house and up to her bedroom for the next hour and they would never be missed.

"He's ours to keep, Dad, right?" Blake was down on his knees getting his face licked.

"He's sleeping in my room," shouted Dalton as he tried to muscle his way in on the action.

"He is not. He's sleeping in mine."

Luke chuckled. "He's sleeping in the mudroom, and there'll be no more arguing over where Ozzie sleeps." Luke turned his head and softly whispered, "Of course, that's assuming he does sleep. This will be his first night away from his mommy."

"Can I teach him tricks, Dad?"

"Can I bring him in for show-and-tell?" Dalton tickled Ozzie's belly and little puppy paws went a mile a minute in the air. "Kyle Olson brought in his iguana last week."

"Can I feed him, Dad?" asked Blake.

"What's he eat?" Dalton frowned. "We don't have any dog food to feed him."

"Yes, we do." Luke nodded toward the truck. "I picked up some in town. I also got Ozzie some other things that he'll be needing."

Blake ran over to the truck and looked into the bed. There obviously wasn't anything exciting to look at, because he raced back to the puppy. "What kind of dog is he, Dad?"

"Ozzie's an Australian Shepherd. He's a working dog."

WIFE IN NAME ONLY   163

"But, Dad, we don't have any work for him." Dalton allowed Blake a turn at scratching Ozzie's tummy.

"He doesn't need work." Luke chuckled and pulled Sue Ellen over to the maple tree and slowly sat down, bringing her with him.

The cool grass was soft beneath her as she continued to watch the boys and the puppy. The sun was shining and the temperature would be hitting the high sixties by this afternoon. Spring had not only arrived in Wild Rose, it was at its crowning glory. She stretched out her legs and relaxed. Luke had been listening to his sons and their, sometimes not so subtle hints about getting a dog.

He was a wonderful father. Then again, she had always known he would be. It was just lately he seemed to be more involved with the boys. When they had first gotten married Luke seemed to stand on the outskirts of his family, being their provider and their protector. He had always been there, but now he was taking the time to relax with his sons. Luke was taking the time to enjoy his sons and the little things in life.

She hoped she had something to do with the changes. But even if she didn't, she'd take them. She was mostly content with the choice she had made. She had gotten her dream, a family of her own. No one ever said the world was a perfect place. What did it really matter that her husband was still in love with his first wife? His dead first wife. The ghost of the perfect Tiffany still haunted the Walkers' home. What other reason could there be for Luke to spend his nights in her bed in the spare bedroom?

Why haven't they ever made love in the master bedroom? Tiffany's pink-and-white, appalling, feminine room. The memories of his life with Tiffany must still be strong and have the power to either hurt or move him. Either way it meant the same thing—Luke was still in love with Tiffany, and he couldn't or wouldn't diminish the memories by making love to another woman in that frilly shrine.

How was she to compete with a ghost, and a perfect ghost no less? Why was it becoming so important that she did compete? She was afraid she knew the answer to that one. She had always been attracted to Luke; she would have had to be living under a rock for the past twenty years not to have noticed him. What she felt for Luke went deeper than just a physical attraction. She had done something which she had sworn she wouldn't do. She was falling in love with Luke.

It was indeed an imperfect world. She was falling in love with her husband. A husband who couldn't love her back because he was in love with a ghost.

"What's wrong?" Luke cupped her chin and forced her to face him. "Don't you like the puppy?"

"I believe I will end up loving Ozzie, as soon as the boys let me near him." She turned her head and placed a kiss in the center of his work-roughened palm. "It was a wonderful surprise, Luke."

"So why such a long face? You looked awfully disappointed there for a moment." Brown eyes that could turn near black with passion were now intently studying every expression on her face.

She silently prayed that Luke couldn't see the truth on her face. The last thing she wanted was his pity.

She tenderly reached out and ran the tip of one of her fingers down the rugged curve of his jaw. "I was just thinking about tonight and Ozzie."

"What about Ozzie?" Luke's brown eyes darkened as he captured her hand and pressed it against his lips.

"Since tonight will be his first night away from his mom and whatever brothers and sisters he had, he'll be lonely." White, even teeth nipped playfully at the base of her thumb. She wiggled her hips and tried for a more comfortable position.

"He had five brothers and sisters." Luke held her hand and teased the tips of her fingers as he counted. "One, two, three, four"—his lips captured and his tongue teased the top of her thumb—"and five."

She gave up trying to find a more comfortable position. It was impossible, unless she was naked, in bed, and with Luke directly on top of her. "Ozzie will be lonely tonight." Her thumb skimmed his lower lip. "One of us will probably have to sleep downstairs with him."

Luke shook his head and grinned. "I don't think so."

"You don't?"

"Nope." Luke's grin turned wicked.

"How are you going to stop Ozzie from being lonely?" That grin reminded her of last night, after the boys were in bed. Luke had disappeared into his office to catch up on some work and she had taken him a cup of coffee and a piece of cherry pie she had baked earlier. Luke had that same grin on as he locked his office door and then proceeded to undress her. Needless to say the coffee was stone-cold before either of them came up for air.

"My plan is simple." Luke brushed his lips over the rapidly pounding pulse in her wrist. "The boys are going to tire that poor puppy out so much, he'll sleep until noon tomorrow."

She glanced over to where the boys were rolling on the ground. Ozzie was jumping on, over and between the giggling boys. "You might have a good plan there, but I'll reserve my judgement 'til later."

"Oh, ye of little faith." Luke clapped his hands real loud and Ozzie came barreling toward them. The puppy was running so fast that it actually tripped over its own front paws twice before making it up onto Luke's lap. Luke scratched behind Ozzie's ears. "Ozzie, old man, I would like you to meet the lady of the house, Sue Ellen."

Ozzie actually looked at her and panted. She reached out her hand to the dog. "Hello, Ozzie. Nice to meet you." Ozzie licked her hand.

Blake and Dalton came running over and plopped down next to them. "Hey, Dad, why did you call Ozzie over here? We were playing with him."

"Ozzie needed to meet Sue Ellen. She's the one who will be taking care of him while you two are in school and I'm outside working all day." Ozzie curled up into a ball in the middle of his lap and closed his eyes. "Besides, puppies need plenty of rest." Luke's fingers were gentle as they slowly stroked the puppy. "See how exhausted he is just from that little play?"

"Oh." Dalton frowned at the dog. "Will he always be that tired?"

"No. He's only seven weeks old. He'll get stronger every day, and by the end of summer he will be running circles around both of you boys." Luke gave Sue Ellen a half-apologetic smile. "Australian Shepherds are known for their high energy level and intelligence. We're going to have our hands full with this one. Do you mind?"

"No. I don't think Blake or Dalton are cut out for some lazy old lap dog." She reached over and ruffled Blake's hair. "These boys definitely need a dog who can keep up with them and accompany them when they go on adventures."

"Adventures?" Dalton's eyes grew wide with wonder. "Did you hear that, Dad? Mom says we get to go on some adventures with Ozzie."

Luke smiled at his sons. "So I hear." With a turn of his head, he faced her again. "You're not one of those types who puts sweaters and little booties on dogs when the weather gets bad, are you?"

Just by the tone of his voice she could tell she would have one heck of a battle on her hands if she ever started crocheting doggie sweaters. "No, but I'm not adverse to getting one of those bandanas for Ozzie, once he gets a little bit bigger. He'll look cool wearing a red one around his neck while riding in the back of the truck."

"Yeah, Dad. Bandanas are cool." Blake looked longingly at the sleeping puppy. "Can we wake him up now?"

"No, let him sleep for a little while longer." Luke's smile widened. "You'll get to tire him out after dinner. I want him to sleep through the night."

* * *

"Mom, I told you I can handle this." Sue Ellen grabbed the bowl containing what was left of the mashed potatoes out of her mother's hands. "You sit down and relax."

"Mothers don't relax. Haven't you figured that out by now?" Her mother continued to clean off the kitchen table and put everything onto the counter. "You get the job of finding room for the leftovers."

Sue Ellen knew it had been a hopeless battle, but she had to at least try. Her mother wasn't happy unless she was doing something. It had always been like that and she guessed it always would be. "Fine, but after this is all put away we're enjoying a cup of coffee either on the front porch or out on the deck."

"That sounds wonderful, dear."

Sue Ellen noticed how her mother was walking halfway around the kitchen just to pass the window by the sink. She was keeping her eye on the boys, her grandsons. It wasn't as if Blake and Dalton would be getting into any mischief. Luke and her father were outside with them, along with Ozzie. Her father had taken one look at the puppy and fallen in love. "I think you need to get Dad a puppy for his birthday."

"Goodness, that's all we need at our age." Her mother brought the last of the dishes over and was reaching for the washcloth.

"Mom, I hate to break this to you, but fifty isn't old." She finished dumping the remaining peas into a plastic container. "You and Dad need something besides dust balls running through the house."

"There are no dust balls in my house." Her mother looked indignant. "Have you ever seen a dust ball in my house?"

"Nope, not even a little dust bunny." She chuckled at the look on her mother's face. "It was a joke, Mom."

"Well, it wasn't funny." Her mother frowned at her. "Have I ever joked about your housekeeping?"

"No, but you do make some nasty cracks about my green thumb." She opened the dishwasher and started loading in the plates.

"That's because you don't have one." Her mother gave her a superior smile, as if she had just topped her, and headed for the herb plants on the windowsill. She tested the soil with the tip of one of her fingers. "You're watering them too much."

"Last week you said I wasn't watering them enough."

"Well, I wish you would make up your mind on how you plan on killing them. The poor things don't know if they should wilt or just turn brown." Her mother's gaze wasn't on the plants. It was focused on whoever was outside.

"Mom, Blake and Dalton are fine out there. They play out there all the time."

"I know that, dear. I wasn't watching them."

Sue Ellen continued to load the dishwasher. She was glad she had invited her parents to dinner. This was the first time they had actually gotten together for a meal since the wedding. Luke needed to see that her parents were a far cry from Evelyn and Frank. If ever there was an opposite of Evelyn, it was her mother. "I told you that Dad really likes that dog."

"I wasn't looking at your father." Her mother turned away from the window and started to wipe down the counters.

"Who were you looking at?" Sue Ellen walked over to the window and peered out. She didn't know anyone else was here. Luke and her father were standing by the driveway, talking and watching the boys ride their bikes. Ozzie was being his usual high-energy self. He was everywhere.

"Your husband."

"You were checking out Luke?" Hey, she really couldn't blame her mom. Luke was indeed worth the time to be checked out.

"I must tell you, Sue Ellen, that maybe I was wrong."

"About Luke?"

"No. I've known Luke since he was born. He's a good, dependable, hardworking man. No one could say a thing against him."

She had to agree with her mother, but the man she just described sounded boring and dull. Luke was neither. "So what were you wrong about?"

"Your marriage." Her mother looked embarrassed but determined. "When you first told me you were marrying Luke, I had my doubts. I figured he was marrying you so his sons could have a mother and the house a keeper. The whole town knew how hard Evelyn had been riding him."

"So why did you think I was marrying him?" Her mother had always had the amazing ability to see things clearly. Her marriage to Luke wasn't one of the things she wanted her mother to see too clearly.

"Loneliness"—her mother shrugged—"maybe out of a sense of responsibility for the boys. You are their godmother, and I knew you took that seriously."

She readjusted two of the pots in the dishwasher because she didn't want her mother to see the truth plastered all over her face. Her mother had been right on the money. "So, what made you decide that you were wrong?"

"You're in love with him, and he's in love with you."

She was curious as to how her mother had come to that conclusion. "How can you tell?"

"The way you look at him." Her mother rinsed out the dishrag and neatly folded it across the faucet. "There's love in your eyes."

"Is there, now?" She gave her mother a small smile and closed the door to the dishwasher. "How can you tell Luke loves me?" She really shouldn't have asked, but curiosity was getting the better of her. Maybe her mother was seeing something she wasn't.

"When he walks into a room, he looks for you immediately. At first I thought he was looking for the boys, but then I realized it was you he was seeking."

"And that proves he loves me?"

"No, it's his expression once he spots you that's so telling." Her mother gave a romantic sigh. "He relaxes."

She walked over to the sink and started to make a fresh pot of coffee. "That explains it." She measured the grounds into the filter basket and chuckled. She had never heard anything so preposterous. "Luke loves me because he relaxes." Only her mother could come up with something so strange.

"Sue Ellen, is something wrong?" Her mother nervously started to rearrange the paper napkins in their basket. "You know I'm not one to interfere, but I'm always here for you if you need something."

"Nothing's wrong, Mom." She poured water into the coffeemaker. "I'm just marveling at your logic, that's all."

Her mother nodded. "Your father and I have never seen you this happy. Motherhood suits you."

She had a feeling she knew what her mother was going to ask next. It was a question she was dreading more and more. *So when are you and Luke planning on adding to your family?* She had never told her mother the reason Ron had ended their engagement. No one knew but Ron and the gynecologist. Her mother wanted grandchildren. The best she could offer were two stepgrandsons. With Evelyn and Frank being the boys' biological grandparents, it was awfully hard on her parents to step into their role. She didn't know how to tell her mother that she had better put her hopes of "real," biological grandchildren on Carrie.

With trembling fingers she reached for the coffee mugs in the cabinet above the coffeemaker. "Carrie called last night."

"She did? That's nice." Her mother busied herself by positioning a silk flower arrangement in the center of the now clean kitchen table. "What did you two talk about?"

Most of what she and Carrie had talked about

couldn't be repeated to their mother. Carrie had been filling her big sister in on her "love" life. Big sister, in return, had been cautioning Carrie to slow things down, and if she wouldn't listen to that advice, to at least use protection. "Oh, nothing much. The same old stuff." Sue Ellen set the four mugs on a tray along with the sugar bowl and creamer. "She said something about not being able to come back home until Christmas. Maybe you and dad should think about flying out there this summer for a visit."

"To Los Angeles?"

"That's where she lives." Her parents never took what she would call a real vacation. Heck, her mother had never been on a plane. "You can go see Hollywood and Beverly Hills. Maybe you can even rent a car and drive down to Mexico for a day or two."

Her mother got a faraway look in her eyes. "I've always wanted to see the Pacific Ocean."

She never knew her mother had dreams of oceans. "Do one better, Mom."

"What's that?"

"Stop in and visit Carrie for a few days and then hop a plane for Hawaii. You'll be surrounded by the Pacific then."

"Hawaii? I've always wanted to see Don Ho. I love his song about tiny bubbles."

Sue Ellen poured the coffee and then picked up the tray. With a wide grin, she said, "Go for it, Mom."

Luke picked up the clean pieces of the carburetor of his tractor and carried them over to his workbench. The steady rain outside was the perfect excuse for ripping apart the carburetor and finally figuring out what was making it stick. Thankfully, all it needed was a good cleaning. His step was light and he started whistling a Garth Brooks song as he reassembled the parts.

Life was good. In fact, life really didn't get any better than this. He had one woman to thank for it all: Sue Ellen Fabian Walker, his wife and lover. What in the world had he ever done in this life to deserve such an incredible woman? She was a wonderful mother to his sons, a fabulous cook and every man's dream lover. The amazing part was that she was all his. Sue Ellen should have been snatched up and married years ago. So why hadn't she made some other man's life heaven on earth?

He knew about her broken engagement to Ron Clemant. What he didn't know was the reason why it had been broken. Currently, there were some strange speculations going around town. He abhorred gossip, so he hadn't really been paying much attention. Their hurried and unexpected marriage had caused old rumors to surface once again. And Evelyn St. Claire wasn't helping matters.

He had no idea what Evelyn hoped to accomplish by stirring up old rumors and gossip. Ron was now a happily married man with one child and another on the way. Sue Ellen was now his wife and the mother of his two sons. Whatever Sue Ellen's or Ron's reason for breaking the engagement, it was personal and belonged in the past.

Lord knew he had carried around the weight of

the past on his shoulders. Sue Ellen was entitled to some privacy and not to be bothered every time she went into town with a thousand questions or stares. He pretended not to notice anything unusual whenever he went into town with her, but he had eyes and ears. He saw the looks and heard the whispers. Most folks didn't mean any harm; they were just curious. Wild Rose was a typical small town, where everyone knew everyone else's business. When there was a secret, everyone's curiosity level skyrocketed until the mystery was solved or some new piece of gossip grabbed everyone's attention.

Evelyn had started all of it with her nosy questions and speculations. Why? Was Evelyn trying to dig up some dirt on Sue Ellen to prove to her lawyer that she was an unfit mother? Or did Evelyn hate Sue Ellen that much for taking her daughter's place? The sad truth was, if Tiffany had been the kind of mother and wife Sue Ellen was, she would still be alive and there would have been no place to fill. Maybe he had made a mistake when he hid the truth about Tiffany from her mother.

Maybe he had made a lot of mistakes in his past, but he wasn't about to make another one now. The next time he saw Evelyn they needed to have a nice long talk. Sue Ellen didn't deserve to be the center of Wild Rose's gossip mill. His wife pretended not to notice or care, but he knew she was hurt by all the talk.

By now all the hoopla over their rushed marriage should have died down. Instead it was worse. The rumors of Sue Ellen being pregnant had died a natural death weeks ago. Now everyone was curious as to why the wedding had been so unexpected and rushed. Within weeks of announcing their "pretend" engagement, they were standing at the altar repeating their vows. Their hasty marriage was unheard of by Wild Rose's standards. Hindsight showed Luke that they should have waited a couple more months before actually getting married. Evelyn wouldn't have been able to gain custody of the boys in that short period of time. But he had been scared so spitless that he was going to lose his sons, that he had pushed for a quick wedding. And Sue Ellen was paying the price for his mistake.

Just as Tiffany had done. He had failed his first wife when he didn't insist she get the treatment and help she needed for her drinking problem. He had begged and pleaded, but he had never insisted. Part of the reason was that he didn't know what to do if she refused him. What was he supposed to do with a grown woman—ground her, take away the television or her Visa card? The other part of the reason, and a very small part, was the fact that he resented it to all hell that he had to police his own wife. That Tiffany had cared so little about him and her own sons that she had literally drunk her life away.

The night Tiffany had died had been Luke's ultimate failure. He had helped bathe the boys and get them into bed because Tiffany had been complaining that he never helped with them, that all he cared about were cornstalks and soybeans. It was the same old argument, only that night Tiffany had been drinking. He hadn't known where she was getting the booze because two nights before he had found and smashed her secret stash. Instead of confronting her and getting into another screaming match, he had gone into his office to catch up on some paperwork. Usually when Tiffany had too much to drink, she fell asleep in front of the television or locked him out of the bedroom.

That night had been different. It had been Dalton's cries that had him rushing from the office to confront his drunken wife and his terrified son in the kitchen. Tiffany was trying to leave the house carrying the struggling and screaming Dalton, who had been only four at the time. Tiffany's ranting about getting a divorce and splitting everything, including the children, had only terrified the boy more. He had tried to reason with her, but she had been too drunk.

Tiffany had headed out the door with the car keys in one hand and a sobbing Dalton in the other. Dalton's little arms were reaching out for him and his screams for help had filled the kitchen. In an error of judgment he would regret to his dying day, he had grabbed his terrified son. By the time he went after Tiffany she was already in the car, heading down the driveway as if the hounds of hell were on her tail.

He had called the sheriff, Sam Burton, to report that Tiffany was not only drunk, she was now behind the wheel of a car. The call had been too late. Tiffany never even made it into town that night. She had lost control of the car only three miles from the farm. The head-on collision with a telephone pole had killed her instantly. Sam had agreed to withhold Tiffany's blood alcohol level from the press and her grieving parents. Knowing the truth about their daughter wouldn't bring her back.

Two weeks after he buried Tiffany, Luke found the nearly empty bottle of Jack Daniel's beneath the kitchen sink. He had failed the woman he loved throughout their marriage and the birth of their children. He had failed Tiffany when he didn't insist that she get some help. He had failed his wife and the mother of his children that fatal night when he grabbed Dalton instead of the car keys.

The sound of Ozzie's barking pulled him from his dark thoughts. He couldn't change the past, but he could make sure he never failed anyone ever again. Blake and Dalton were his main concern, and now there was Sue Ellen to worry about. At first Sue Ellen was just a convenient mother to his sons. The boys needed a mother, so he got them one. Now she was something more, something deeper. Sue Ellen was family.

Ozzie raced into the barn, quickly followed by Blake. "I beat you both!"

Dalton and Sue Ellen ran through the big open door at a dead even tie. Sue Ellen sucked in some air and grinned. "So who's the rotten egg now?"

"Not me," shouted Dalton. "We were tied. Right, Dad?"

He smiled at the sight of his family. They were splattered with raindrops and grinning like a bunch of lunatics. "It looked pretty even to me." He bent down and petted Ozzie, who was dancing around his feet demanding attention.

"Okay, so there's no rotten egg this time," muttered Sue Ellen. "I'll get you next time."

Dalton just smiled smugly and followed Blake to the other end of the large building. Ozzie took off barking after the boys.

"What are you going to do when he gets faster?" He loved the flush sweeping up her cheeks and the sparkle of life in Sue Ellen's beautiful blue eyes. She was more than just family; how much more he didn't want to hazard a guess. Falling in love with Sue Ellen hadn't been part of the plan.

"I'll tie his shoelaces together." Sue Ellen took another gulp of air and tried to steady her breathing.

"That would be cheating." He glanced off to the other end of the barn, where the boys were climbing on the tractor and taking turns sitting in the seat.

"You think it's fair now that a six-year-old boy can practically beat me in a race from the porch steps to the barn?"

"All you need to do is toughen up a bit." His gaze traveled the length of her body. From the clinging, damp T-shirt to the skintight faded jeans. He remembered the intense pleasure he had gotten the other night in his office, when he had pulled those tight jeans off her long legs. There wasn't an inch of her incredible body he would like to see toughened up.

"How do you recommend that I toughen up?"

"I could chase you around the bed a few more times every night."

Sue Ellen softly smiled and shook her head.

He arched an eyebrow. "No?" That sweet, soft smile of hers went directly to his gut.

"I could never run from you."

He groaned and glanced down to the other end of the barn. The boys were watching them. "You're going to pay for that comment later."

The soft smile turned wicked. "I'm counting on it." A sweetly curved hip leaned against his workbench. The enticing smile faded away and a serious look took its place. "I need to discuss something with you."

"What?" He put down the screwdriver and gave her his undivided attention. Sue Ellen rarely complained or made inane remarks. It was one of the small things he appreciated so much about her.

"Blake and Dalton are planning something."

He quickly glanced at the boys. They were huddled together on the seat, whispering. "How can you tell?"

"The secret whispering to each other has been going on all morning." Sue Ellen shifted her weight. "I've been expecting a rubber snake to jump out at me or something just as diabolical."

He rubbed his jaw in a fruitless attempt to hide his smile. "Whispering, huh . . . sounds positively evil."

"Laugh all you want, but I heard your name whispered once or twice."

Another quick glance confirmed that the boys were indeed looking directly at him. "Okay, my curiosity is piqued. What do you think they're up to?"

"It's hard to tell. At first I thought they were planning some practical joke. Now I'm not too sure. Whatever they've been discussing, it seemed pretty important."

"Who's discussing it more, Blake or Dalton?"

"Blake's doing most of the talking. Dalton seems to be reassuring him about something."

"Do you think it's about Ozzie?"

"No, it's about you, or me, or even the both of us together." A fiery blush swept up Sue Ellen's cheeks and her gaze was locked on the far wall. "You don't think they heard us last night, do you?"

Understanding came swiftly, as did his grin. "You mean when you screamed?"

"Lucas Albert Walker, I swear . . ."

"Hey"—he held up his hands in mock surrender—"how was I to know you would scream when I touched my tongue there?"

It seemed impossible, but her blush grew brighter. "You should have thought of that before you . . . you . . . you know what!"

He felt desire shoot through his body like a lance. The final target was one very uncomfortable spot behind the metal zipper of his jeans. "You're assuming that I can actually think when I'm making love to you."

"You don't think when we're making love?" Sue Ellen tilted her head and studied him.

"Oh, I think, all right." He stepped closer and outlined her lower lip with the pad of his thumb. "But not about the boys sleeping across the hall, corn yields or what Ozzie might be getting into at the moment."

"What do you think about?"

His grin was slow in coming and his voice dropped to a low growl. "Making you scream."

Sue Ellen took a step closer but immediately

jumped back as Dalton's voice shattered the moment. "Mom, Dad, can we talk to you?"

He glanced at the boys as they came running, with a barking Ozzie at their heels. Lord, he prayed they hadn't heard Sue Ellen scream last night. How in the world was he ever going to explain that one? A mouse in her room held possibilities. "Sure, boys, what's up?" He knew what had been up last night. Six- and eight-year-olds didn't need to know that particular fact of life quite yet. His gaze couldn't meet Sue Ellen's.

Dalton nudged his older brother forward. "Blake needs to ask you a question. I told him it would be okay, but he doesn't believe me."

The fact that Dalton, who was younger by two years, was directing his older brother didn't go unnoticed. Dalton had always been the more outgoing one. Blake had a tendency to hang in the background and silently observe. Blake looked extremely nervous. Luke's gut was telling him that this wasn't about last night's scream. "This sounds important, Blake." He knelt down so that he was on eye level with his son. "What do you want to ask?"

Blake shuffled from foot to foot until Dalton gently elbowed him in the ribs. "I want to know if I can call Sue Ellen 'Mom' too." The toe of one of Blake's sneakers tried digging a hole in the concrete floor of the barn. "Dalton does it, so I was wondering if I could, too? I know she's not my real mom and all, but . . ."

Luke shot Sue Ellen a quick glance. She looked to be stunned—but happily so. He didn't blame her. He felt the same way. He had set out to find a mother for his two sons, and it looked like he had succeeded better than his wildest dreams. Both of his boys had opened their home and their hearts to Sue Ellen.

He understood Blake's hesitancy in coming forward with this request. Blake had only been six when Tiffany had died, but he still had memories of her. Time had erased most of Dalton's memories of Tiffany. Family photos, videos and Evelyn kept the memory of Tiffany from fading completely. Thankfully, the nightmares that had plagued Dalton from that fatal night had also faded and disappeared over time. For months after his mother's death, Dalton had horrifying nightmares of being dragged off to heaven with his mother. Luke had almost gotten professional help for Dalton, but with love and reassurances the nightmares became less and less frequent until eventually they were gone.

Luke reached out and hugged Blake and smiled at Dalton. "You both know that your real mother is in heaven."

Both boys nodded.

"Your mom knew how important it was for little boys and big boys to have a mom. She was the best mom she could be, while she was with us. She loved you both so very, very much." He opened his arms wider, and Dalton slipped into his hold. "But she's been gone a very long time."

"And she can't come back." Dalton's voice held the maturity of a six-year-old who had all the answers.

Luke released his sons. "That's right." He ruffled Dalton's black hair, so much like Tiffany's, and then he mussed Blake's light brown hair, so much like his own. The memories he held of Tiffany might not all be pleasant, but every one of those was shadowed by his love for his sons. Tiffany had given him the most precious gifts imaginable. For that, he would never blacken her memory to her sons. "What have I always told you your mother would want you to be?"

Both boys answered together. "Happy. Our real mom would want us to be happy."

"That's right." He looked at his youngest son, who looked so much like Tiffany, from his black hair to his crystal blue eyes. "Does it make you happy, Dalton, to call Sue Ellen 'Mom'?"

"Yes."

His gaze moved to Blake, who was the spitting image of himself at that age. He had the photos to prove it. "Would it make you happy to call Sue Ellen 'Mom'?"

"Yes."

Luke turned and glanced at his wife. Tears were pooled in her eyes, but she was valiantly holding them back. "What about you, Sue Ellen? Would it make you happy if both the boys called you 'Mom'?"

Even white teeth caught her trembling lower lip and she quickly nodded. Luke didn't think she could utter a sound if her life depended on it. Good thing it didn't. "Well, it's settled then. Sue Ellen, you are now the proud mother of two growing boys who think chocolate chip cookies are a food group."

Ozzie came scooting out from underneath a hay wagon to join the group. The puppy had managed to find something sticky to roll in and hay clung to every inch of his fur. Everyone burst out laughing at the comical sight. Ozzie looked like a demented, yapping tumbleweed.

"Hey, Dad, does that make her Ozzie's mom, too?" Blake was grinning as he looked from the puppy to his mom.

"In a way, I guess it does. Why?" He chuckled at the puppy, who seemed to like being the center of attention.

"I vote for Mom to give him the bath this time."

NINE

Sue Ellen glanced in the backseat and smiled at the boys. Both were bouncing with anticipation for the night to come. Wild Rose's annual spring festival was right down the road, and the night held nothing but the promise of great food, fun, games and an enjoyable evening filled with family and friends. The festival was all the boys had talked about all week long. The only down side to the evening was that Ozzie couldn't accompany them.

The puppy was confined to the mudroom with more puppy toys than he knew what to do with. The huge basket she had bought to hold all the toys was overflowing, and there were more puppy playthings scattered through every room of the house, along with slobbered-on socks and one of Luke's good dress shoes chewed beyond hope. Ozzie was a one puppy chewing machine. The good news was that Ozzie was now housebroken and, for the most part, slept through the night.

Luke was the culprit behind the invasion of rawhide bones, squeaky neon alien heads, rope pulls and

WIFE IN NAME ONLY 187

a plastic chewable mailman. The man couldn't run into town without coming home with something for Ozzie. The puppy was spoiled rotten and had all three males eating out of his paws. Sue Ellen prided herself on being made of stronger stuff. She had only bought one can of tennis balls. The whole-grain and cheese doggie cookies she had baked the other day didn't count as spoiling the puppy. They were a nutritious snack, not something for Ozzie to play with.

"Remember, boys, we're going to eat dinner before we start to play the games."

Both boys rolled their eyes and grinned. "Yes, Mom."

"Hey, Dad, can I try dunking the principal of our school? He told us that he'd be in the dunking booth tonight." Blake's voice held excited anticipation and confidence.

"You can try." Luke chuckled as he continued to drive toward Wild Rose. "Any man crazy enough to get into one of those dunk tanks deserves to go swimming."

"Can I try for a goldfish, Mom?"

"I guess, but where are you going to keep it if you win one?" Goldfish? What did she know about taking care of a goldfish? Not much. Sprinkle some food into the bowl and change the water occasionally. Sounded simple enough.

"I've got some birthday money left. I could buy a fishbowl and keep it up in my room."

"Sounds reasonable to me," Luke said. "Why don't we wait and see if you win any goldfish first?"

Luke glanced at her. "You're not opposed to fish in the house, are you?"

"No, but I draw the line at piranhas." It was sweet of Luke to ask her opinion on goldfish in the house, but she wasn't surprised by the gesture. Luke was incredibly sweet. He also was incredibly sexy. It was an enticing combination. Was it any wonder she had fallen in love with him? Weeks ago she had convinced herself that she was falling in love with her husband. Now she knew it was a bunch of hogwash. She was in love with her husband; there hadn't been any falling involved.

Luke reached over and placed his hand on her knee as the boys laughed. Strong fingers lightly played with the long, flowing flower-print skirt she had chosen to wear to the town's annual event. Wild Rose's spring festival consisted of games and booths set up by various organizations and plenty of food and music. There would be dancing later on for the adults, and free baby-sitting for the kids at the local Methodist church. She had never danced with Luke before and was looking forward to the experience.

"What about a snake, Mom? Can we get one?" Blake's question pulled her thoughts away from being in Luke's arms and sent a shiver of fear racing through her entire body.

Luke must have felt her stiffen, because he reassuringly patted her knee. "There'll be no snakes or any other reptiles in the house."

"What about an iguana?" asked Dalton.

She wanted to field this one. "We'll discuss iguanas once you're old enough to take care of an animal like that. I think you both need to learn the responsibility of taking care of Ozzie first, before you turn the farm into a zoo." She placed her hand on top of Luke's and gave it a small, triumphant pat. She thought she'd handled that very well.

Luke turned his hand over and laced his long fingers with hers. "I think your mother is right, boys. Ozzie and the possibility of a goldfish are about as far as we go right now."

She gazed from her husband's handsome profile to the scene of passing houses. She didn't want Luke to see the sheen of tears in her eyes and get the wrong idea. The way Luke referred her to the boys as "your mother" caused her heart to flutter and expand. She could actually feel it grow within her chest. It was so full of love, it was nearly bursting.

Being someone's mother was so natural, so common. Millions, probably billions of women every day were called "mom" and thought nothing of it. Yet to her it was a miracle. The boys accepting her as their mother was one thing. Blake and Dalton were young enough to want a mother, and it was easy for them to transpose that want and need into a reality. Luke was a different story. Luke had married her to give his sons a caregiver. Love and hearts had nothing to do with it, then. Now was a different story.

Love and hearts had everything to do with it now. They were a family now. The only way it could get any better was if Luke actually loved her back. Oh, he physically desired her and was a thoughtful and energetic lover. His mere kisses had the power to melt her bones and stop her heartbeat. When they made love, to her it was making love. Her body, heart and soul were involved. She didn't know what it was for Luke. It seemed to be more than just sex and the urge to satisfy some adult need when he joined her every night in her bed. The way he touched her felt like love, so why didn't he say the words?

Why was the master bedroom still a shrine to Tiffany? She had personally redone or at least changed every room in the house—except the master bedroom—since their marriage. The boys needed a home, not an elaborate showcase of a house. The Walker home was now a comfortable, country-feeling home. It once again fit into the surrounding cornfields. Except for the master bedroom, the room she was too scared to ask Luke if she could change. Changing the room didn't scare her. Some of her ideas were perfect for the room, and for Luke. But she hesitated to bring the subject up to Luke because she was unsure of his reaction. Luke might take it as her pushing her way into the last corner of his life. But the real fear was that he would refuse to allow her to touch the room. Then she would have to confront the truth, and all the hope that was burning in her heart would surely die. Luke could never love her because he was still in love with Tiffany.

"Wow, Dad," Blake said, "look at all the cars."

"It looks like everyone in this part of the county is here." Luke pulled the car over into the first available space. "We're going to have to walk from here."

Blake and Dalton had scrambled out of the car and were impatiently waiting on the sidewalk before Luke even finished talking.

Sue Ellen chuckled as she unbuckled her seat belt. "I don't think walking a couple of blocks will be a problem."

Luke pulled Sue Ellen closer and allowed his feet to slowly shuffle back and forth to the beat of the music. He hoped it was to the beat of the music. With Sue Ellen all warm and tender in his embrace, it was hard to concentrate on anything else but the feel of her body and the scent of her flowery perfume. This was the first time he had ever danced with Sue Ellen, and had he known what an erotic experience it was going to be, he would have done it long ago. He also would have picked a more private location, preferably one with a bed close by. As it was, half the adult population of Wild Rose and the surrounding area were crammed together on the street in front of the Wild Rose National Bank. The country band the town had hired was set up on the marble landing in front of the main doors to the bank.

The spring festival committee had really outdone itself this year. White Christmas tree lights were strung everywhere, giving Main Street and the town's square a fairy-tale quality. The game booths were now closed and the children had all either been sent home or taken to the social hall in the basement of the Methodist church. Blake and Dalton had been settled in the social hall for the past half hour. There were cots available for the children who got tired, but he didn't think either of his sons would use one. Both were too cranked up to sleep.

Blake had managed to get off a lucky shot and had been the only kid going into the third grade next fall to actually dunk their principal. This feat had earned him a couple of slaps on the back, a demand from the little league coach for him to come to practice next Tuesday afternoon and a group of giggling girls that had followed him everywhere. He was secretly impressed with the pitch his son had thrown but didn't want to make a big deal about it and become one of those sport-fanatic fathers. On the other hand, he had no difficulties seeing Blake as the starting pitcher for Wild Rose High's varsity baseball team in another nine years.

Dalton had not only managed to win a goldfish, he had won four. That cute little goldfish bowl he had been planning on seeing on his son's desk had suddenly turned into a ten-gallon aquarium with a filter, lights, colored rocks and probably a scuba diver hunting buried treasure. He would have been worried about the school of fish Dalton had won, except every time his son had managed to throw a Ping-Pong ball into one of the small glass fishbowls to win a fish, Sue Ellen had screamed with delight. He hadn't figured out who had been prouder of the achievement, his son or his wife.

He felt Sue Ellen's mouth press a kiss to the side of his throat and groaned as a flash of desire streaked to his groin. The sheriff and his wife, Annie, danced inches away. Sam, the sheriff, looked over his wife's head and looked directly at him and raised an eyebrow. He managed a stiff smile and turned Sue Ellen to a less crowded corner of the street. "You're going to pay for that one."

Sue Ellen smiled against his throat. "How am I going to pay?" She ran her hands up his back and toyed with the hair at the back of his neck.

"You're going to have to walk around in front of me for the rest of the night." He moved his hips slightly against her so she wouldn't be in any doubt as to the reason why. Her sweet laughter went straight to his heart. He pulled her closer. "You think it's funny?"

Sue Ellen glanced up, and a soft smile turned up the corners of her mouth. "I think it's appropriate."

"Appropriate?" He lowered his head and softly whispered, "One teasing kiss and I turn as hard as stone? How is that appropriate?"

"Your kisses do the same to me." Her teeth playfully nibbled on his ear. "Except I don't turn hard, I get all hot and empty inside."

His feet stopped moving and his breath refused to leave his lungs.

Sue Ellen glanced at him. Concern darkened her eyes. "Luke?"

He sucked in some air and managed to pull her to the edge of the dance area. "Are you ready to leave?" He ran his hand through his hair and felt moisture break out across his neck. Damn, he wanted his wife, and he wanted her now. It wasn't a really warm night, but he was sweating now. Sue Ellen had already pulled on the sweater she had brought with her.

"No." She twirled around him like some playful fairy, and he felt the soft silken folds of her skirt wrap around one of his legs. "I want to dance some more with you."

"We can dance at home. There's a stereo in the family room." With her long, flowing hair and her sparkling blue eyes reflecting the hundred tiny white lights strung everywhere, she reminded him of a fairy, a beautiful, tempting fairy. The only things missing were the wings.

"I want to dance with you under the lights. There's magic in the air tonight, don't you feel it?" She held out her hands and charmed him with her soft, inviting smile.

He pulled her back into his arms and turned slowly toward the dance floor. "What I'm feeling right now, sweetheart, has nothing to do with magic." If Sue Ellen wanted to dance some more, who was he to refuse her? He'd dance with her the entire night if that's what she wanted to do. His overactive hormones could just find something else to do for the next couple of hours. He pulled her closer and whispered, "If you want to dance, behave yourself."

"I promise to behave"—she straightened the collar on his shirt—"for now."

Luke smiled into the darkness and held her close. He noticed all the other couples dancing nearby and had to wonder if any of them were as happy as he was at that moment. He doubted it. No one could be as happy as he was with Sue Ellen in his arms. He watched as high-school sweethearts and couples that had been married for over fifty years danced by. He knew most of them by name. Wild Rose was a close-

WIFE IN NAME ONLY 195

knit community, and he had observed the courtships, the weddings and the births of the next generation.

A small frown pulled at his mouth and threatened to ruin his mood. He'd just realized that he never had an actual date with his wife. There had been no courtship period, where he had wooed her with flowers, dinner dates and jewelry. There had been no backseat makeout sessions at the local drive-in. They had never shared a root beer float at Garfield's. He had never won her a stuffed animal at the Harvest Day Fair or bought her a birthday present. Hell, he hadn't even gotten her an engagement ring. She wore a simple gold band and had never asked for more.

His feet faltered and he nearly stepped on her toes. "When's your birthday?"

"The end of the month. Why?" Sue Ellen raised her head off his shoulder and looked at him.

"What day?"

"The twenty-third."

"What would you like?" Lord, it was only two weeks away.

Sue Ellen chuckled and put her head right back on his shoulder. "I don't want anything. I have everything I want."

"Come on, give me some suggestions, a hint even." He had never bought a woman a present before without a detailed list in his hand. Tiffany had always handed him a list of possible presents at least a month before any major holiday or event for which she felt entitled to receive a gift. Tiffany's list not only included the name of the item but the store where he could find it, the size and the name of a salesclerk, in case he was too stupid to read. He'd hated those lists.

"A cake; you can get me a chocolate cake, Luke." Sue Ellen's chuckle warmed his shoulder.

"I've got to get you something besides a cake."

"Surprise me, then." One pale pink painted fingernail toyed with a button on his shirt as the song came to an end. "I love surprises."

"Okay, folks," cried the lead singer of the band, "we're going to liven things up a bit."

Luke pulled her off to the side. He could manage not to make a fool of himself slow dancing, but he drew the line at anything faster than a foxtrot. "How about if I go get us something to drink?"

"Sounds great." Sue Ellen nodded to the street where everyone was lining up. "I'll be right here watching Muriel and Ruth line dance."

Muriel and Ruth Wentzel were eighty-one-year-old identical twins, and between them, they had the distinct honor of going through seven husbands. Both were keeping their eyes open to see if they could add to the number. He chuckled as he brushed a kiss across her cheek. "Okay. I'll be right back."

Sue Ellen watched as Luke threaded his way through the gathering crowd and softly sighed. Lord, he was a handsome devil. Maybe she should have gone with him. She shook her head and chuckled at her silly jealous thoughts. Luke had married her. He was her husband, and to Luke that was a lifetime commitment.

The crowd and the line dancers increased in number, and she stepped off the street and up onto the

WIFE IN NAME ONLY

grassy square. She backed up, so she had a better view of the dancers, and ended up against a mass of trees and shrubs at the corner of the square. A familiar figure joined the crowd in front of her, but he hadn't seen her. Ron Clemant, her ex-fiancé, was less than three feet away from her.

She debated for a moment, and then softly called his name. "Ron?"

Ron turned around and hesitantly smiled. "Sue Ellen?"

She understood exactly how he felt. She and Ron had managed to keep their distance from each other over the years. Oh, they passed each other on the street occasionally, or they would meet at some large gathering, like this festival, but a simple nod or greeting had been all they said to each other. Tonight she wanted to say more. She motioned him over with a wave.

Ron glanced around him before stepping farther into the shadows. "Hello, Sue Ellen. You're looking good. Marriage must agree with you."

"Thank you." Ron seemed nervous, so she gave him her most friendly smile. "Luke just went to get us something to drink." Maybe Ron would relax if he knew Luke was coming right back. She had gotten over her infatuation with Ron years ago. She knew now that what she had felt for Ron was a deep friendship that had come at a time in her life when she had started to dream about a family of her own. Ron, who had a similar dream, had been the obvious choice to fulfill that dream. The dream had ended when she'd learned that her chances of ever conceiving a child were about the same as hitting the state lottery. Ron had been the one to end the engagement. At the time, she had been more heartbroken at the news she would never have a child than at Ron's betrayal.

"I hear you and Cindy are expecting your second child this fall. Congratulations."

Ron appeared startled. "Thanks."

She gave a weary sigh. What was Ron expecting her to do? Rant and rave about how he'd broken their engagement then gone out and married another woman and started a family? "Listen, Ron, I know this is awkward for us both. So I just want to say there are no hard feelings on my part. You did the right thing years ago, and I wouldn't be totally honest if I told you I would have stuck by you if you had been the one who couldn't have children."

"Really? You would have broken the engagement if things were reversed?"

"Probably." She wasn't proud of that fact, and the question had been eating at her for years. Would she have ended the engagement? "At that point in my life, having a family of my own was very important to me."

"Now you have one." The stiffness went out of Ron's shoulders. "Luke's a great guy."

She grinned. "Yes he is, and his sons—I mean, *our* sons—are wonderful."

"Then it all worked out for the best."

"Yes, it did." Sue Ellen glanced around to make sure they weren't being overheard. What had happened between them years ago wasn't anyone's business. "There is one other thing. . . ."

"What's that?"

"Evelyn St. Claire isn't real happy with my marriage to Luke. She feels it's a threat to Tiffany's memory, since I stepped into the role of mother to her grandsons."

Ron rubbed the back of his neck. "Yeah. I've been hearing things to that effect."

"She's been trying to find something in my background that would deem me an unfit mother. The only black mark, if you will, is our broken engagement. Since only we know the reason, there's a lot of speculation floating around."

"I'm not proud of what I did, Sue Ellen, but if you want me to, I'll talk to Evelyn and explain how it was I who acted like a jerk. From what I hear, you're a wonderful mother to those boys." Ron reached out and gently squeezed one of her hands. "Evelyn should be counting her blessings that her grandsons have someone like you to love them."

"Thank you, Ron." Damn, tears were filling her eyes. "I don't want you to talk to Evelyn. It's none of her business. It was between you and me, and it's all in the past. Evelyn can't harm me because there's nothing to harm me with." She turned her hand and returned the squeeze. "I was worried about how Cindy was handling having your name dragged through the rumor mill. Expectant mothers shouldn't have unnecessary stress."

"Cindy's as healthy as a horse and glowing. She's not worried about something that happened years ago. She knows I love her." Ron seemed to be studying her face. "Are you truly happy, Sue Ellen?"

"Yes." She reached up and brushed a kiss across his cheek. "Things really do work out for the best."

"See!" cried Evelyn St. Claire. "I told you, Luke."

Sue Ellen turned and watched as Evelyn dragged Luke forward. What appeared to be soda was spilling out of the two cups Luke was holding. A dozen people, who had been standing nearby, had turned toward them when Evelyn cried out.

"She was kissing him!" Evelyn's glare was triumphant. "You saw her kissing him. I know you did."

She could feel Ron stiffening beside her, but she continued to look at her husband. Luke had seemed bewildered for a moment, but now he appeared perfectly relaxed. Luke handed her one of the cups. "It's Coke. They ran out of Sprite."

Luke turned to Ron and stuck out his hand. "Hi, Ron. I haven't seen you in a while. How have you been?"

Ron shook Luke's hand. "Fine, just fine."

Evelyn's face turned so red, even in the shadowy darkness it appeared to be on fire. "Luke, what are you doing? He's the man your precious little wife was just kissing!" Evelyn's breath was coming in great gulps and she had worked herself up into a state. "You never should have married her, Luke. She can't replace Tiffany. She's not half the woman my daughter was!"

A hush fell over the crowd, and it seemed to Sue Ellen that even the band had turned down its volume. She wanted the earth to open up and swallow her whole. Here she had been, trying to avoid or at least defuse the situation and look what she'd caused. Wild Rose would be feeding off this encounter for months.

Luke slowly turned and faced his ex-mother-in-law. His voice was low and dangerous. His face was a blank mask, hiding his fury. "If you ever say one more word against my wife, I will personally make sure the only visits you have with your grandsons are supervised." There was a collective gasp from the few people close enough to hear Luke's threat. "I won't have you poisoning their minds against their new mother. Blake and Dalton love Sue Ellen as their mother. She is my wife, and will stay my wife."

Luke took a weary breath and watched Frank St. Claire make his way through the crowd to join them. "Tiffany is gone, and no one is sorrier for that loss than I am. She's not coming back, Evelyn. Life goes on. Accept it."

Evelyn had tears streaming down her face, but instead of looking crushed and grief-stricken, she appeared to be furious. Luke shook his head and looked at Frank St. Claire. "Take her home, Frank, and try to make her understand that this has gone on long enough. I won't tolerate it any longer."

Frank took his wife's arm and started to lead her away.

"One more suggestion, Frank . . ." Luke said.

"What?"

"Counseling. Get her some grief counseling."

Sue Ellen gently tucked the covers up to Dalton's chin and then placed a kiss on his cheek. He sighed in his sleep but didn't open his eyes. Blake was already tucked in and asleep in his own bed. Luke was downstairs handling four goldfish and a wired-up Ozzie, who had been thrilled to see them come home from the festival. Luke had been anything but thrilled when they left town. He had barely spoken three words to her since the confrontation with Evelyn an hour before. She was getting scared.

She glanced at her youngest son and gently brushed a lock of black hair from his smooth forehead. He never even flinched. The sleep of innocence. She continued to look at him as she walked to the doorway and turned off the light. Her eyes and heart watched the gentle rise and fall of his small chest for a moment more before she stepped into the hall.

She nearly screamed as she bumped into Luke. She hadn't heard him come upstairs. Her hand went to her heart. "Lord, Luke, don't sneak up on someone like that."

"Sorry." Luke took hold of the hand she had pressed against her chest. "We need to talk."

She swallowed hard. "Okay." Her feet stumbled a step as Luke led her into the master bedroom. Tiffany's room.

Luke flipped the light switch, tugged her the rest of the way into the room and softly closed the door.

She had thought she was scared before, with Luke's silence. Now she was terrified. Luke had never brought her in here before. Occasionally she dusted the room, and she put away Luke's laundry, but that was about it. There was no cause to change the sheets anymore because Luke hadn't slept in the bed for weeks. She watched in silence as Luke prowled the room. He looked at everything but her.

WIFE IN NAME ONLY 203

Her heart sank. Luke had listened to Evelyn's words and was now realizing that she had been right. Sue Ellen Fabian could never replace Tiffany St. Claire.

Luke prowled his way back to her. He stood directly in front of her, glanced around the room, shuddered and then said, "I hate this room."

She blinked. "What did you say?" He couldn't have said what she thought he had.

"I said that I hate this room." Luke gave her an intense look before asking, "Don't you think there's something strange about a husband and wife sleeping in the spare bedroom instead of the master bedroom?"

She slowly nodded. "I thought you liked this room the way it is."

Luke's laugh didn't hold one ounce of humor. "What in the hell ever gave you that idea?"

"You didn't change it after Tiffany's death."

"I didn't change anything after she died, did I?"

"Why didn't you?"

"Mrs. Johnson, the housekeeper I hired, thought the entire house was perfect the way it was. Since I didn't know the first thing about decorating, I just left it alone." Luke glared at the pink wallpaper. "Why didn't you offer to redo this room? You've redone the entire house, making it feel like a home instead of some museum or an advertisement in some glossy magazine. Yet you stubbornly refuse to touch this room. Why?"

She glanced around and saw Tiffany in everything. "I figured this was the room where you would have most of your memories of Tiffany. It's a private room between a husband and his wife. I know what you and Tiffany had was very special and that you loved her greatly. You two had the perfect marriage." She felt her throat start to close up with tears and she quickly glanced away from Luke.

"So you thought what? This room was some kind of shrine to Tiffany?"

Her "Yes" was whispered to the floor.

Luke took her hand and led her over to one of the delicate little chairs. His hands were gentle as he pushed her into the seat. He took a few steps to the bed and sat down facing her. "Tiffany wasn't as perfect as everyone thought."

She raised her gaze. Luke appeared to be serious. "Oh, I know. No one is perfect, but you have to admit Tiffany came pretty close." What was Luke going to tell her, that Tiffany had drooled when she slept, burned a pot roast or got cranky during her time of the month?

"I don't like to speak unkindly of the dead, especially since they aren't around to defend themselves. But I think we need to clear up a few things." Luke rubbed his jaw for a moment and thought. "Tiffany was a spoiled brat. She was the homecoming queen who never grew up."

Sue Ellen kept her jaw from dropping open by sheer determination. She couldn't say a word if her life depended on it.

Luke gazed directly at her and said, "She was jealous of everything and everyone, and I killed her."

TEN

Sue Ellen's jaw dropped open on that one statement. There wasn't enough determination in the world to prevent it. "You killed Tiffany?"

"I might as well have. I failed her that night, and she died."

"Back up, Luke. Tiffany died in a car accident. She was the only occupant of the car and you were three miles away, at home here, with the boys. So, tell me again how you killed her." Luke wouldn't harm a soul, especially his first wife. There was no way she could believe any of this.

"Let's start from the beginning. Tiffany was a closet alcoholic. For the last two years of her life, she was drunk most of the time. During the day she was pretty good and rarely drank. At dinner time she started to eat less and drink more. In the beginning I tried to help around the house as much as possible and do little things to make her feel special.

"Tiffany needed to be the center of everyone's attention, and she wasn't any longer; the boys were. Everyone doted on the boys, and I couldn't make up for the loss. When she started drinking more I begged and pleaded with her to get some help. She refused. I used to search the house every time she had gone out and pour her supply of booze down the toilet. It became a constant contest to see how much she could buy and hide and how much I could find and dump."

My God! Sue Ellen had no idea that Tiffany had had a drinking problem. No one knew. She would bet every cent she had in the bank that Tiffany's own parents hadn't known. Luke obviously wasn't telling her everything, nor did she want to know every detail of their marriage. That one simple sentence said it all: *Tiffany was a closet alcoholic.* "What happened the night she died?"

"She hid a bottle of Jack Daniel's under the kitchen sink. I didn't find it. She was feeling good by the time I came in from the fields. By the time the boys were in bed she was drunk. I figured she'd pass out on the sofa, which she usually did, so I went into my den to do some work. The next thing I heard was Dalton screaming. By the time I reached the kitchen she was halfway out the front door. In one hand she had the car keys, in the other Dalton. He was only four years old and he was so scared. He had no idea what was happening. He was holding out his arms to me and crying."

She left the chair and knelt at Luke's feet.

"I failed her that night."

"How?" The anguish on Luke's face tore at her heart. How could Tiffany have done this to her family?

"I grabbed Dalton out of her arms instead of the car keys. By the time I got Dalton calm enough to release his stranglehold on my neck and head outside for Tiffany, she was gone. I saw the red taillights as she turned onto the main road. I called Sam Burton, the sheriff, and told him that she was drunk and driving toward town, but it was too late. She never made it into Wild Rose."

"Oh, Luke, you didn't fail her. She failed herself and her family." Sue Ellen reached up and pulled him into her arms. His powerful body trembled within her embrace, and she tightened her hold.

"I should have grabbed the damn keys."

"No, you did the right thing, the only thing. A father's instinct is to protect his children, and that was what you did when you grabbed Dalton." She pressed herself onto his lap and slowly ran her hands up and down his back. Twenty months was a long time to hold all of this illogical guilt inside. Luke had nothing to feel guilty about, but she understood him enough to realize why he did. Luke was a natural-born protector. He would see it as a failure that he hadn't prevented the accident. In his own way he was still protecting Tiffany. She didn't know how he had convinced the sheriff not to release the fact that Tiffany had been intoxicated that fateful night, but she wasn't surprise that he had done it.

"Luke, listen to me." She pulled back so she could see his face. "Tiffany was twenty-five years old. She was a wife and a mother of two very small boys. She chose to drink. You weren't holding the bottle to her mouth and forcing it down her throat." There was so much pain in Luke's eyes. Pain that pierced her own heart.

"I failed her, Sue Ellen. Don't you see?"

She pushed herself off his lap and stepped away. "No, I don't see. How did you fail her? Weren't you a good husband? Were you a lousy father to her sons?" She waved her arm to encompass the entire room and the house beyond. "Didn't you provide very well for her and the boys?" She could see Luke's jaw tighten, but she continued to hurl questions at him. "Didn't you love her enough, Luke?"

Luke's face crumbled and he looked away. "No, I didn't love her enough. Maybe if I had she wouldn't have drunk." He clasped his hands between his knees and stared at his shoes. "It gets very hard to continue to love a self-centered drunk."

"But you did, didn't you?"

"Yes, but obviously not enough. She was my wife and the mother of my sons."

"And now?" Luke had loved Tiffany the night she had died. But did he love her still? Sue Ellen held her breath and waited for his reply.

Luke's response was a long time coming. He seemed to have shaken off the past memories and his small smile was genuine. "Now you are my wife and the mother of my sons."

No words of love. What was she expecting, a declaration of love and devotion? She quickly glanced away so Luke wouldn't see the disappointment on her face. A gold frame photo of Tiffany was the first thing she saw. Tiffany appeared to be laughing at her. "I'll redo this room, if that's what you want." She would take great joy in stripping every last reminder of Tiffany from the room.

Luke stood up and pulled her from the room. "The hell with the room, Sue Ellen." He tugged her into the hallway and kissed her deeply.

She melted into the kiss and wrapped her arms around him as if she would never let go. A groan of frustration left her lips when he broke the kiss.

"What I want right at this moment is you." Luke picked her up, carried her into her bedroom and deposited her in the middle of the bed. Her skirt and hair floated around her. Laughter and desire darkened his eyes as he locked the door and started to unbutton his shirt. "I told you, you'll pay for teasing me on the dance floor."

She softly smiled and held out her arms. She might not have her husband's love yet, but the hope in her heart was building faster than the desire racing through her body. The old insecurities, her fears of never being able to match his perfect memories of Tiffany were gone. Tiffany and their marriage hadn't been so perfect after all.

Luke's shirt hit the floor. "Did I tell you that you looked beautiful tonight?"

She watched as his pants joined the shirt. "It was all those little lights strung around the town." Her breath hitched in her throat at the sight of his naked body. His aroused naked body. She swallowed hard. "It gave everything a romantic glow."

Luke slowly shook his head and smiled as he ran his fingers up her nylon-clad legs. "It reminded me of fairy tales." Her skirt was being bunched across her thighs. "And you, my lovely, were the tempting fairy queen."

"What was I tempting you to do?" Warm fingers teased the inside of her thighs and she silently cursed the inventor of panty hose.

"You'll see soon enough." Luke's grin held nothing but a wicked promise as he lowered himself on top of her.

A long time later Sue Ellen lay in Luke's warm embrace and slowly regained her breath. If that was what Christmas lighting did for her husband, she was heading up to the attic first thing in the morning and pulling down the lights she had stashed up there.

Luke's arms tightened around her. "You okay?"

She smiled. "You don't have to sound so damned pleased with yourself when you ask that question."

Luke chuckled and a kiss landed on the top of her head. She snuggled closer and allowed contentment to wash over her. She was nearly asleep when it was pulled away by her straying thoughts. "Luke?"

"Hmm . . ." Luke sounded as if he was on the verge of falling asleep himself.

"You never asked about Ron. Don't you want to know what you and Evelyn interrupted?"

Luke was slow in answering. "If you want to tell me, I'll listen."

She frowned into the darkness of the room. If she had found Luke and an ex-fiancée lurking in the shadows of the town square, she would be very interested in knowing what was going on. Luke didn't appear to be interested at all. "I was congratulating him on the impending birth of his second child." She waited for a heartbeat to see if Luke would ask a question. When he didn't she finished her explanation. "I was also making sure that his wife wasn't getting upset with all the rumors Evelyn had a hand in starting again. Expectant mothers have enough to contend with, without adding Evelyn into the equation."

"I take it that Ron and Cindy are fine, despite Evelyn's meddling?"

"Yes." She waited a moment before adding, "The kiss you saw me brush across his cheek was a congratulations, best wishes, good-bye gesture. That's all."

Luke's arms tightened for a moment. "Good."

She waited for him to say something else, but he didn't. It took her a couple of moments to realize that he had fallen asleep. *That was all he had to say about it—good!* Didn't he even want to know why Ron's and her engagement had ended? Not that she particularly wanted to tell him that story, but he had the right to know. After all, she was his wife now.

The hope that had been building in her heart started to waver. If Luke loved her, he would be demanding answers, wouldn't he? What did he feel for her, then? Was it just plain lust that she had been sugarcoating for her own justification?

The steady beat of Luke's heart beneath her ear should have been comforting. It wasn't. The night seemed a little bit darker and colder. Her thoughts a little more depressing. It was a long while before she managed to fall into an uneasy sleep.

***

Luke stood in the shadowy doorway of the barn and watched his wife work on her vegetable garden. She had poured her heart and soul into that little fenced-in plot, and boy, did it show. She was going to be able to feed a small Third World country by the time she was done harvesting everything she had planted. This morning his wife looked like an adorable, sweaty garden fairy.

He was tempted to sneak up behind her and tease her into making love in the cool shade under the maple tree. The boys were in school, and Dalton wasn't due home for another hour or so. The only one who would see them in their birthday suits doing the wild thing was Ozzie. He didn't think Ozzie would care too much. The only thing stopping Luke was that he wasn't 100 percent sure of the reception he would get from Sue Ellen.

Something was bothering her. No matter how many times she said nothing was wrong, he didn't believe her. Ever since last week, and the encounter with Evelyn at the festival, something had been playing heavily on his wife's mind. He couldn't tell if it had been Evelyn's behavior or the discussion they had had later that evening about Tiffany and the night she had died. Whatever it was, it wasn't agreeing with his wife, and he didn't like that at all.

He wanted Sue Ellen deliriously happy, or at least as happy as he was. Oh, she still smiled and laughed with the boys, but the spark in her beautiful blue eyes seemed to have dulled a bit. He caught her staring out windows at nothing in particular, and she'd almost started crying the other night when she burnt the chicken for dinner. It hadn't been that burnt, and he had eaten an extra helping just to show her how much he enjoyed it. He would have eaten the darn thing raw if it would have stopped those tears.

Sue Ellen still welcomed him into her bed and her arms every night. Their lovemaking had never been hotter. He didn't know how it was possible, but it seemed to get better with every new night. Her gentle touch not only aroused his body, but soothed his soul and moved his heart.

Her birthday was three days away, and he already had her present bought and hidden in the glove compartment of his truck. Talking to Sue Ellen about Tiffany had not only lightened the load he had been carrying on his shoulders, it had shown him something else. Maybe he hadn't failed Tiffany as much as he'd thought. Maybe Sue Ellen was right; Tiffany had failed herself and he had been caught in the downward spiral. For the first time in years his heart felt lighter, and with it came a remarkable discovery: He was in love.

He loved Sue Ellen. She was everything he had always wanted in a woman and a wife. Once he had admitted that to himself, what he would be getting her for a birthday present had been preordained.

There could be one other explanation for her recent behavior. Sue Ellen could be pregnant. That possibility had occurred to him two nights earlier and last night he had, in a roundabout way, questioned Sue Ellen about it. She had been lying in his arms, exhausted and totally satisfied, if her contented sigh had been any indication. He'd casually asked her about birth control, and if she was using something. Sue Ellen had stiffened, but she hadn't uttered a word. He had tenderly rubbed her abdomen, kissed the top of her golden head and told her not to worry; what happened, happened.

Birth control had never been an issue when they had first gotten married; she was going to be his wife in name only. Now, he would love to see Sue Ellen grow round and proud with his child. He loved his sons totally, but a daughter or even another son would find plenty of love within their home and their hearts.

Sue Ellen must not have taken his words to heart, because she hadn't made any startling announcements. Then again, maybe she didn't know for certain, or maybe she wasn't pregnant at all and he was just grasping at straws. He hadn't seen any home pregnancy tests lying around, nor had she been tossing up her cookies in the mornings.

He watched in silence as Sue Ellen stood up and stretched the kinks out of her back. Desire pooled in his groin as her blouse tightened across her breasts. He released the breath he had been holding as she picked up the basket filled with hand tools and walked toward the house. Ozzie followed loyally at her heels. A moment later she was gone from his sight, but not from his heart.

There were only three days left before Sue Ellen learned exactly how much he did love her.

* * *

WIFE IN NAME ONLY   215

Sue Ellen impatiently tapped her fingers against the steering wheel and glared out the windshield at Evelyn's empty house. The house where her sons should have been twenty—she glanced at her watch for the hundredth time—twenty-four minutes ago. Evelyn knew she was coming at ten-thirty. It was now nearly eleven, and Luke would be worrying soon. She would have called him, but the cell phone was in his pickup and not her car. It probably wouldn't have done any good anyway even if she had the cell phone with her. Luke was probably out in the barn, making sure everything was ready in case the storms that were predicted did strike. Spring storms were unpredictable and violent.

The boys had spent last night with their grandparents, and Sue Ellen had called Evelyn early that morning and explained about the weather forecast, and that she would be there at ten-thirty. So where were Evelyn and the boys?

Luke had wanted to pick up the boys, but she had convinced him that she could handle Evelyn. Yesterday afternoon, when Evelyn came to pick up the boys, had been the first time she had seen or spoken to the woman since the festival. Evelyn had been distant yet polite. Sue Ellen had taken it as a good sign.

Luke hadn't been as generous in his assessment of his ex-mother-in-law. Her husband was still furious about the show Evelyn had put on at the festival.

She stared at the darkening skies and wondered if she could get away with wringing Evelyn's neck. After all, today was her twenty-eighth birthday and she was entitled to one wish, wasn't she?

This morning she had given herself one little secret wish. It wasn't going to be a secret for very much longer. She had spent over an hour moving all of Luke's clothes into her bedroom. She hadn't asked his permission, but then, how could he expect her to redo the master bedroom if she didn't empty it out first? There had been more than enough room for his clothes in her closet, and she liked seeing them hanging there. She was tired of seeing him run back and forth between rooms. It wasn't any way to conduct a marriage. Luke not only belonged in her bed but in her room.

The hard part of the morning had come when she started packing up Tiffany's photo gallery of herself. Tears had filled her eyes as she studied each picture. Tiffany had been the girl who had it all: beauty, wealth, a loving husband and two adorable boys. Why couldn't she have found happiness and contentment? Why had she turned so self-destructive? So many questions, and all without answers.

She had dried her eyes and placed a picture of Tiffany holding each of the boys in the their bedrooms. Blake and Dalton should each have a picture of their real mother. If they ever wanted to put away the picture, it would be their choice, not hers or Luke's. The rest of the pictures she left in their frames, wrapped them carefully in newspaper and took them to the attic. She had commandeered a huge black steamer truck in the attic as Tiffany's. In it she placed items of Tiffany's that the boys, or even Luke, might want in the future. It was a sad tribute to a woman who had given her so much. Tiffany had

WIFE IN NAME ONLY

given her her family, and for that she would be eternally grateful.

She spotted Evelyn's flashy Cadillac coming down the street and got out of the car. She wasn't eternally grateful to Tiffany for leaving her her mother, though. The woman could try the patience of a saint. She walked to the front of the house as Blake and Dalton tumbled from the car, all smiles and legs. "Hi, Mom!"

She smiled and hugged the boys. "Hi, yourselves." She nodded to the house. "Why don't you two hurry and get your bags. I want to get home before the rain starts."

Evelyn unlocked the front door, and the boys disappeared inside. "I just had a very *interesting* conversation." Evelyn's voice sounded smug and triumphant.

Sue Ellen didn't have time to discuss interesting conversations with Evelyn, nor did she want to. She tried to keep the impatience from her voice, but she knew she failed. "Some other time, Evelyn. We've got to be going." By now, Luke would really be worried. The boys and she should have been home fifteen minutes ago.

Blake and Dalton came running back out of the house, each carrying his own bag. "Say good-bye to your grandmom, boys. We have to hurry."

Evelyn kissed the boys and said her good-byes. "Go wait in the car for Sue Ellen; she'll be right there."

Sue Ellen turned away from Evelyn and started walking back down the driveway to her car. Blake and

Dalton were scrambling into the backseat. She didn't want to get into it with Evelyn now.

"I talked to Cindy Clemant this morning."

Sue Ellen's feet halted and she turned around to face Evelyn. She heard the car door shut behind the boys. "Leave Cindy alone and out of any problems you might have with me, Evelyn. She doesn't need any added stress; she's expecting."

"Something you will never be able to achieve." Evelyn's blue eyes and painted mouth hardened.

"What are you talking about?" Sue Ellen's gut already knew what Evelyn was talking about, but she squared her shoulders and faced the woman.

"You're barren! You can never have children of your own, so you hoodwinked Luke into marrying you." Evelyn's voice rose and her face turned a brilliant red. "You wanted my grandsons for your own and you stole them from me!"

Sue Ellen felt every ounce of color drain from her face as she slowly shook her head. Tears clogged her throat, but she couldn't utter a sound.

"I'm telling Luke!" Evelyn's body trembled with her rage. "I'm telling Luke that the only reason you married him was because of the boys."

She slowly turned, walked to the car and drove away. Evelyn's cries were still filling the air.

"Mom, what's Grandmom yelling about?" Blake was twisting around to see out the back window.

Dalton was struggling against the seatbelt to get a better look. "I've never seen Grandmom so mad. What did you say to her?"

Sue Ellen blinked away the tears filling her eyes

and concentrated on driving. "Nothing, honey. It's just a misunderstanding." She turned off Evelyn's tree-lined street and headed out of town. "We'll work it out later. Everything will be fine." Lord, talk about pushing the envelope of hope.

She needed to talk to Luke before Evelyn did. It would be better if she, not Evelyn, was the one to tell him why Ron had broken the engagement to her years ago. Luke had the right to know that his wife was barren. Maybe it wouldn't matter to him. He never mentioned having or wanting more children.

But what if he did?

The skies went from gloomy to an angry, rolling gray as she turned onto the main road that would eventually lead to Luke and their farm. The clouds above them seemed to twist and turn into a huge angry mass. The boys grew quiet in the backseat, and she remembered the other night, when Luke had mentioned birth control. She had been so panic-stricken that she hadn't uttered a sound. Luke had kissed the top of her head and said something about what happens, happens. That night his big, callused hand had gently caressed her abdomen all through the night. God, what would happen if Luke really did want more children? Children she couldn't give him.

She was so distracted with her thoughts of Evelyn and Luke that she didn't notice the worsening storm until it was practically on top of them. Within a heartbeat she went from being distracted to pure terror. She had been born and raised in Iowa and wasn't any stranger to storms and the dangers they held. The dense dark clouds above her and the eerie greenish tint to the sky revealed the warning signs that this storm contained something she'd never wanted to see or experience—a tornado.

Sue Ellen quickly glanced around her. She already was miles out of town and there was nothing close by but open fields. Acres and acres of knee-high cornstalks surrounded her. Not another car was on the road. She was alone with two boys in the backseat.

"Wow, Mom, do you see the sky?" Blake's voice held awe and maybe a touch of panic.

"How come it's green, Mom? I thought skies were only blue?" Dalton seemed more curious than scared.

She was scared enough for everyone.

She bent forward and studied the sky as she kept the car heading forward. A funnel formed in the distance before she could take her foot off the gas pedal and decide if it was safer to keep heading for the farm and Luke, or turn around and head back to town.

Both boys shouted as the funnel extended downward toward the fields. Common sense told her that she couldn't outrun it. The road only gave her one direction in which to head, and her car could never outrun a twister across a cornfield. The safest course of action was to get out of the car, find a ditch and lie flat until the danger had passed.

Her only thought was to protect Blake and Dalton as she quickly scanned the area. The slight indentations at the side of the road were barely noticeable and wouldn't offer her or the boys much protection against the fury of nature. A quarter mile up the road was an overpass. A small creek ran beneath the road and a few trees bordered the creek that cut through a field. She pressed on the accelerator, covered the distance in record time and then slammed on the brakes while yelling at the boys to unbuckle their seat belts.

She threw open her door and was reaching for the back door when golf-ball-size hail started to pound into her. She grabbed each of the boys' hands, yanked them from the car and ran for the side of the road and the creek. Dirt skidded beneath their feet as they slid and tumbled down the incline, heading for the creek and hopefully the safety of the overpass.

She slipped and felt a gash slice into her calf, but she didn't bother to look to see how much damage had been done. Rule number one: when running from a tornado, wear jeans and sneakers, not shorts and open-toe sandals. If she didn't get the boys to safety, who would care about a small cut, or even a large one?

Hail pounded into her back and on top of her head as she tried to protect the boys with as much of her body as she could. Blake was yelling something, but the wind was whipping the sound away too fast for her to understand what he was saying. Dalton's arms were trying to cover his head and his ears. The wrath of the tornado was tremendous. It sounded like a freight train barreling down the tracks. The sound alone was paralyzing her with fear. She didn't need to see the funnel to know she was up against one of nature's mightiest furies.

Her hair whipped across her face, stinging her

cheeks until tears formed in her eyes. She blindly pushed the boys under the overpass and away from the hail. With one last glance over her shoulder she saw the twister ripping through the cornfield, heading straight for the road and them. Cornstalks, dirt and anything else within its destructive path was being torn up and whipped around with ungodly force.

She scrambled in under the overpass. Her heart sank when she saw how little room or protection the concrete pillars holding the road above the creek were going to offer them. There was barely enough room for a family of hamsters, let alone two scared boys and their mother. But beggars couldn't be choosers, and this was all she had to work with.

She hurriedly pushed the boys up and under as far as they could scramble. She hardened her heart as they cried out as rocks and dirt bit into their tender flesh. She'd take them bruised and cut, as long as they were safe and alive. When they were pressed as far back as they could go, she stretched out in front of them, offering them as much protection as she could. Rocks, dirt and assorted garbage cut into her skin, but she ignored everything, concentrating on keeping the boys as safe as possible.

Dalton was squeezed in between Blake and herself with his face pressed against her stomach. Blake was directly behind his younger brother, with his back against a slab of concrete and his face pressed against her throat. She could feel his tears. Both boys wanted to wrap their arms around her, but she forced their arms down into a more protected area. Her back was the most vulnerable to flying debris. The overpass should hold together. Flying debris was going to be their biggest worry.

"Mom!" cried Dalton above the roar.

"It's okay, Dalt. I'm here." She wrapped one of her arms above Blake's head and pressed him closer. Her other arm she squeezed into the area between the boy's body and the concrete form above them. Some of the skin on her forearm was scraped raw, but she needed to hold her sons more than she needed the skin. Her trembling fingers found the belt loops on Blake's shorts and she threaded her fingers into them and held on tight.

She was worried about Dalton being able to breathe, but if he was crying out, he was breathing. "Close your eyes, both of you." She shouted into the fury and prayed they could hear her over the pandemonium. "It will be over in a minute."

As the debris pummeled her back and her bare legs she prayed for the boys' safety and for Luke's forgiveness. She had put the boys in this danger by not paying attention to the weather. Luke had told her about the storm, but she had been too distracted by the argument with Evelyn. She should have seen how bad it was and taken shelter in town. Instead she had been so worried about things that couldn't be changed and winning Luke's love that she had put his sons in danger. If something should happen to his sons, she would never win his forgiveness, let alone his love. Then again, if something should happen to Blake or Dalton, she would never forgive herself. She loved them both as if they were her own.

Something slammed into her back and she couldn't

prevent the cry or the jerk of her body. Bursts of lights and black dots danced across her closed eyelids and she sucked in a mouthful of dusty air. Pain rippled into her shoulders and past her hips.

"*Mom!*" cried Blake against her throat. He tried to raise his head.

She tightened her hold and kept his head covered. He must have felt the impact of whatever slammed into her. "I'm fine." Best outcome was one hell of a black-and-blue mark. Worse case, a broken rib or two. She didn't want to take a deep breath to find out.

She felt Dalton press closer, if that was possible. The boy was practically in the front pockets of her shorts already. She moved her legs closer to his. Blake and Dalton had been wearing shorts when she had picked them up from their grandmother's. It was an unseasonably hot day. Their bare legs were being stung by flying dirt and pebbles. She wished there was more she could do for them, but there wasn't.

She heard a horrendous grinding noise over the sound of the tornado and wondered what was making the sound.

After what felt like a lifetime, but in reality was only a moment or two, she felt the fury of the tornado abate. The noise started to fade and the twisting wind started to die down. She gave a silent prayer of thanks. They had made it through without serious injuries.

Cautiously she raised her head and squinted through nearly closed eyes. The first thing she noticed through the swirling dust and flying debris was that a tree had been uprooted and was laying across the creek. Massive roots had pulled from the ground, and branches were everywhere. The twisted remains of the metal guardrail was dangling and whipping wildly from the overpass above them. The hunk of metal was about eight feet away from her head and banging wildly against one of the concrete forms supporting the overpass.

She was turning her head to see if she could spot anything else when a small, five-inch piece of the guardrail came undone and flew directly at her. She tried to duck, but there was nowhere to go. The boys and she were wedged in tighter than sardines. The small chunk of metal connected with the side of her head. She felt the explosion of pain, and then there was nothing but blackness.

Luke stepped out of the barn and frowned up at the sky. The weather forecast had called for some severe storms, and there was a tornado warning posted, which wasn't unusual for this time of year. He didn't like the look of the sky. He called Ozzie, who had been keeping him company while Sue Ellen had run into town to pick up the boys, and hurried for the house.

Sue Ellen and the boys should have been home by now. Why hadn't they come to the barn to get Ozzie? The boys never let the puppy out of their sight when they were home. Luke entered the house at a dead run, calling Sue Ellen's name. Silence. He stood at the foot of the stairs and yelled both of his sons' names. The silence was broken by Ozzie's whine. He hurried to the kitchen window and looked outside. Sue Ellen's car wasn't in the driveway.

He was reaching for the phone when it rang. He picked it up before the ring was even completed. "Sue Ellen?"

"No, Luke, it's Evelyn." His ex-mother-in-law's voice sounded unnaturally high and filled with fear. "Isn't she home yet?"

"If she were home, why would I be asking if it was her on the phone?" Luke ran his hand through his hair. Through the kitchen window he was watching the sky with a sense of dread. "Did she pick up the boys?" He quickly glanced at the clock. Sue Ellen should have been home a half an hour ago.

"Yes." There was a sniffle on the other end. "The Weather Channel just issued a tornado watch for this area, Luke, and I'm scared."

"Of a tornado?" It was on the tip of his tongue to tell her that she had good reason to be intimidated by tornadoes; they had been known to land on wicked witches in the past.

"The sky looks terrible and Sue Ellen and the boys just left." The sniffle turned into a sob. "It's all my fault!"

"What's your fault?" A cold lump of dread settled in his stomach. What was Evelyn blubbering about? He pulled the phone closer to the window. Dark clouds were racing and gathering together at an alarming rate.

"I wasn't here when Sue Ellen came for the boys. She told me about the weather, but I didn't listen." Evelyn's voice was filled with tears and pleas. "I wasn't here and she had to wait. Now Blake and Dalton are out there and there might be a tornado. It's all my fault!"

Luke dropped the phone and ran. The sky wasn't looking funny; it was looking green! He vaguely heard Evelyn shout something, but he didn't stop. He was heading for his truck, scanning the sky in the direction of town, when his heart froze. His feet came to a sudden stop and were riveted to the asphalt of the driveway as a dark funnel cloud descended from the heavens, swept and twisted its way across open fields that separated his farm from town and then disappeared back up into the sky. The road to town—the road his wife and sons would have been on—had been directly in the tornado's path.

He was in his truck, racing toward town before he even knew he had moved. With a trembling hand he reached for the cell phone and punched in the sheriff's number. His eyes scanned the empty road ahead for any sign of Sue Ellen's red car.

"Sheriff's office." The dispatcher sounded half asleep.

"This is Luke Walker. A tornado has just touched down out by the Gardner place. It crossed Olsen Creek Road and then went back up."

"Is anyone hurt?" The dispatcher seemed to come awake in a hurry.

"I'm heading down the road now. I don't see anyone yet." Sue Ellen was a smart woman. She probably saw the sky and headed for her parents' house to wait out the storm.

The cell phone was still clutched in his hand when

he spotted Sue Ellen's car in the distance. A prayer and a curse both tumbled from his mouth.

"Repeat that, Luke." The dispatcher seemed to be getting anxious.

He ignored the phone and drove around a downed tree branch. Sue Ellen's car was sitting sideways across the road. Two of the doors were wide open and one of the back tires was off the road completely. He slammed on the brakes and jumped from the truck yelling Sue Ellen's and his sons' names. His heart slammed against his chest as he looked in her car. It was empty, except for the boys' tote bags and his wife's purse. A rock had been hurled through the front windshield, shattering it and his composure. Panic was clawing its way up the back of his throat. Where was Sue Ellen? Where were his sons?

He glanced around wildly, yelling their names at the top of his lungs. The dispatcher at the sheriff's office was yelling something to him over the phone, but he ignored the demanding voice and concentrated on finding his family.

In the distance, he could hear another voice. A familiar voice. Blake's voice! He started to run toward the creek and the echoing voice.

Both Blake's and Dalton's cries reached him as he slid down the embankment toward the creek and the underpass. It took him less than a minute to locate his sons, and the sight that greeted him stopped his heart. Sue Ellen was lying there, blocking in the boys at the top of the incline, wedged under the supports, and she wasn't moving. One glimpse of her still body and blood-streaked legs told the story. Sue Ellen had used her own body to protect his sons.

He dropped to his knees, crouching down as far as he could to scramble up the small incline. He gently turned Sue Ellen over. Her face was pale and streaked with dirt. A small trickle of blood was seeping from a cut directly above her temple, but she was breathing. He sucked in his first breath since seeing her laying there and glanced at his sons. Both had tear-streaked faces and were covered in dirt, but they appeared unharmed. He pressed his finger against Sue Ellen's neck. Her pulse felt strong and steady.

Blake and Dalton were both talking and yelling at the same time as they moved out of their cramped hiding place. "Is Mom all right?"

"Something hit her and then she went to sleep." Dalton's voice was trembling with tears. "She wouldn't wake up, Dad!"

"There was a tornado, Dad! I saw it!" Blake pushed away from the concrete support and stones started to slide down the incline, straight onto Sue Ellen.

"Easy, boys, don't move yet." He was gently starting to move Sue Ellen into his arms when the sound of the distraught dispatcher, who was still on the cell phone yelling his lungs out, got his attention. He had slipped the phone into his shirt pocket when he needed both hands to turn Sue Ellen over. In all the confusion he had never disconnected the call. He yanked the phone out of his pocket, gave the location and demanded an ambulance immediately.

ELEVEN

Sue Ellen heard the high-pitched whining grow closer, but she tried to push the noise away. She had something very important to do, but she couldn't remember what it was. The loud noise and muffled voices were distracting her. She couldn't think. It hurt to think. It hurt not to think.

She reached for her head, where the pain seemed to be coming from, and groaned as her back protested the movement.

"Easy, love, try not to move." Luke's voice whispered across her cheek as his fingers gently lowered her hand back down to her side. "Help's almost here."

It took her a moment, but she managed to open her eyes. Luke's face came into focus, but it didn't look like Luke's face. It was too pale, and his eyes looked funny. They looked like he had been crying. Why would Luke be crying?

She closed her eyes and tried to think. Luke was pressing something against the side of her head, and it felt like he was using a sledgehammer to do it. What had happened? "Don't"—she reached for his hand—"it hurts."

"Sorry." Luke lowered his hand. "You're awake now."

"Didn't know that I was sleeping." She opened her eyes again and stared at the sky above Luke's head. The sun was peeking through some nasty-looking clouds and off to the right was a pulsating red light. She slowly turned her head and frowned at the blinking lights on top of the sheriff's car. Her car, which was next to the sheriff's, was parked sideways across the road, the back end off the asphalt. In a blinding flash she remembered the tornado ripping through the fields, heading right for her and the boys. She tried to sit up. "Blake? Dalton? Where are the boys?"

"Shhhhh . . ." Luke gently pushed her shoulders back until she was once again lying on the soft grass. "They're fine, Sue Ellen. Sam has them in the backseat of his car."

She looked again at the sheriff's car. Sam was squatting at the rear door, quietly talking to whoever was in the backseat. She couldn't see who it was. "I need to see them."

"Who?"

"The boys." She reached for his hand and managed a small squeeze. "I need to see that they're all right."

"Okay, but they're still pretty shook up." Luke's fingers were gentle as he wiped a soft, wet cloth across her cheek. "Dalton was quite upset that you wouldn't wake up and Blake can't stop talking about how you saved their lives."

She started to shake her head and then thought better of it. Movement caused her too much pain. "He's got that wrong. I should have been paying better attention to the weather. I'm the one who drove them straight into danger." The cool cloth felt wonderful as Luke slowly wiped the other cheek. It was the only thing that felt wonderful on her entire aching body. "I'm sorry, Luke."

"You have nothing to be sorry for." He glanced over at the sheriff's car. "Blake, Dalton, your mom wants to see you both." A smile brightened his face and his eyes. "She doesn't believe me that you both are fine."

Blake and Dalton scrambled out of the sheriff's car and came running toward her. Besides a few scrapes and a thick layer of dirt, they appeared to be fine. She felt the weight that had been pressing on her heart lift. Blake and Dalton were safe and sound.

"Are you awake now, Mom?" Dalton's eyes swam with tears and worry.

She smiled and managed to bite back a groan of pain as she reached her hand out toward her son. "Yes, I'm awake." Dalton grabbed for her hand and squeezed it tight. She concentrated on appearing as relaxed as a person could be with an ambulance screeching to a halt twelve feet away. She got the feeling she was going to be the lucky passenger. "I'm sorry I scared you both."

Blake took her other hand. "Something hit you on the head."

"It felt like a building."

Luke chuckled, a harsh little sound, as he brushed

back her hair and studied the bump above her temple. "I think it was a piece of the guardrail that had come free."

"Good guess, but it still felt like a ton of bricks."

"You hurt anywhere else, besides that and the gash on the back of your calf?" Luke's fingers patted her bare knee. There was a bunch of gauze already wrapped around her leg. "Do you know what hit you there?"

"Nothing; I cut it while sliding down the incline." She tried to smile at the boys, but she had a feeling it was more of a grimace than a smile. "You should be proud of the boys, Luke. They can really hustle when the situation calls for it."

Luke shuddered visibly as he glanced over her and the boys toward the ambulance.

"Something else hit Mom, Dad." Blake's eyes were tearing up again. "I heard her cry out."

Luke raised an eyebrow and stared at her. She rolled her eyes. It was the only movement she could manage. "My back, and no, I don't know what it was." She frowned at the two paramedics as they pulled a gurney out of the back of the ambulance and started for her. Being picked up wasn't on her top-ten list of things she wanted to do right about then. "This isn't going to be fun."

Luke frowned. Sam glanced from the paramedics to Sue Ellen. The sheriff's frown matched Luke's. "Hey, Luke, how about if I take the boys and meet you at the hospital? You can ride with Sue Ellen. I'll have one of my deputies drive your truck over as soon as they're done inspecting the surrounding area for damage."

"Boys, would you like a ride in the sheriff's car? Your mother and I will meet you in the emergency room. I want a doctor to look you both over. Even though you seem to be okay, I want to make sure."

Blake and Dalton looked at Sue Ellen, as if waiting for her to make up their minds for them. "Go; I'm fine. It's not every day you get a chance to ride in the sheriff's car." She glanced up at Sam and forced another smile. She'd known Sam her entire life. "Maybe if you ask real nice he'll let you turn on the siren."

Sam rolled his eyes but nodded his head. "That's all my own kids need to hear, that I let someone else's kids play with the siren." The sheriff nodded to his car. "Come on, you two. Maybe if we hit the siren this far out of town, they'll never find out."

Both Blake and Dalton very gently kissed her cheek. "We'll see you there, right, Mom?"

This time her smile didn't hurt so much. "Right." She watched as they followed the sheriff to his car.

"Hey, Squirt"—Sam turned back to her after closing the door behind her sons—"happy birthday."

Over an hour later she felt 80 percent human again. What the other 20 percent was, she wasn't hazarding a guess. The ride to the hospital hadn't been as bad as she had feared. Luke had been with her, reassuring her and trying to stay out of the paramedics' way.

Luke quietly slipped back into her cubicle in the

WIFE IN NAME ONLY

emergency room. He had been checking on the boys. He gave her a huge smile. "Blake and Dalton are both fine and being thoroughly spoiled by a bunch of nurses. Your parents are out in the waiting room. I've already told them that you're fine and they can see you soon." Luke walked to the side of the bed and kissed her again.

The doctor, who had examined her when she first arrived, pushed back the beige curtain and joined them. He glanced through the paperwork attached to the clipboard in his hands. "Well, Sue Ellen, everything looks good."

She already knew that. The bump and gash on her head hadn't required stitches, but they had shaved a small area surrounding it and used two butterfly bandages to hold the scalp together. The cut on the back of her calf had been deeper, and six, presumably tiny, stitches had closed it. If that was the worst she had suffered, she counted herself extremely fortunate.

"Whatever hit you in the back did a heck of a job. It bruised you pretty good. We want to take a couple of X rays to make sure it didn't crack or break a rib or two. It's just a precautionary measure. We also want a shot or two of your head, just to make sure it's as thick as I'm presuming it is." The doctor gave her his best bedside-manner smile.

Luke chuckled. "I can verify that it's thick all right, but take the X ray just to make sure."

Sue Ellen playfully glared at her husband. "Go ahead, what're a few pictures considering what I've just been through?"

"I'm sure running and hiding from a tornado was

quite an experience." The doctor looked embarrassed at joking with her.

She grinned. "I was referring to all the poking and prodding you guys have done in the last half hour. The tornado was a piece of cake compared to needles, scrubbing, being stripped naked and having my leg sewn back together." It felt good to laugh.

The doctor and Luke both laughed with her.

"Okay, I'll have someone from X ray come get you in a minute. After I see the X rays, we'll settle you in a room for the night. I want you here under twenty-four-hour observation before I release you." The doctor flipped the chart closed. "One last question before the X rays—is there any chance you could be pregnant?"

She looked down at her bruised and scraped hands, laying on top of the blanket they had given her. "No."

Luke turned to the doctor and said, "Yes."

She glanced up at her husband. The hope in his beautiful brown eyes pierced her heart. It was time for the truth. Long past time for the truth. "Can I have a few minutes alone with my husband?"

The doctor glanced from one to the other. "Sure. I'll be back in a little while." His white coat flapped behind him as he disappeared behind the curtain.

"Sue Ellen?"

Her fingers nervously twisted the edge of the cotton blanket. "You never seemed interested in wanting to know why Ron and my engagement was broken years ago."

"I figured it was private, between you and him.'

WIFE IN NAME ONLY 237

Luke sat on the edge of the bed and took her trembling hands in his.

She studied the small sink and cabinet across the cubicle. She was afraid to face Luke, afraid to see disappointment and anger darken his expression. She should have told him before they were married. "I went to a gynecologist for birth control, so there wouldn't be any accidents until we were ready to start a family."

"What happened?"

She blinked away the tears that were pooling in her eyes and took a deep breath. "The gynecologist discovered I have what is known as a tilted uterus. He told me that I have a better chance of hitting the state lottery than I do of ever conceiving a child." There, she had said it. "I would have told you before we got married, but you said we wouldn't be sharing a bedroom, so it didn't matter then."

"Do you think it matters now?" Luke's voice held nothing but tenderness.

"I don't know." She risked a quick glance at him, but he didn't seem angry or upset. "You never said whether you wanted more children." She went back to studying her bruised and scraped hands.

"You're right, I've never said." Luke's fingers were gentle as they cupped her chin and forced her to look at him. "I'm going to say this once, and only once, so pay attention." He leaned forward and kissed the corner of her mouth. "It doesn't matter."

"Children don't matter to you?" She didn't believe him. Not for a moment did she believe Blake and Dalton didn't matter to this man.

Luke slowly shook his head. *"Our* sons mean the world to me and you know it, so don't confuse the issue by trying to put words into my mouth." His hands gently covered hers and pulled the blanket away from her twisting fingers. "If we ever have any more children, they will be as wanted, loved and cherished as Blake and Dalton already are."

She sank her teeth into her lower lip, waiting for him to continue. Luke remained stubbornly silent as he stared at her mouth. She couldn't stand the silence. "What if we don't have any more children, Luke?"

"Then, and only then, it doesn't matter." He reached up and slowly pulled on her chin until she released her lower lip. The pad of his thumb slowly caressed the moist and tortured lip. "Ron was a jerk for what he did to you, sweetheart, but do you know what?"

"What?"

"I'm extremely grateful to the man." He leaned forward, cupped both her cheeks and kissed her senseless. "If he had married you, you would have been his wife, and then *I* wouldn't have been able to marry you."

She smiled for the first time since the doctor had asked if there was a possibility that she could be pregnant. Luke had taken the news very well. Better than she had hoped.

Luke bent his head and kissed her again. The sweet, gentle kiss turned passionate, and she melted into his arms.

A polite cough came from the foot of the bed. Luke slowly released her and grinned. She grinned back.

The doctor was studying the ceiling tile. "I see someone is feeling better—much better."

She refused to blush, but the heat of a flush still swept up her cheeks. She wouldn't look at Luke because she knew he was silently laughing. She could feel the bed shake. "I'm much better, thank you."

"Good." The doctor looked from Luke to her. "I'll ask this once again: Is there a chance you could be pregnant?"

She sat up straighter, stared right at the doctor and said, "No."

Luke shook his head. "Yes."

The doctor rolled his eyes. "Is there something I'm missing here, or do you two need some pamphlets?" His voice held a hint of laughter. "I have some videos I could lend you that might clear up this matter."

Her face felt as if it was on fire. She glared at Luke as he stood up. "I want her to have a pregnancy test, just to make sure, before you bombard her body with radiation."

The doctor nodded his head. "Wise choice."

"Luke?" Tears filled her eyes. Didn't he understand what she had been telling him? She couldn't conceive a child. Why would he want to torture her with a pregnancy test?

Luke pressed a quick kiss on the tip of her nose. "Sue Ellen, someone always hits the state lottery."

Sue Ellen couldn't stop grinning. She was going to have a baby! Correction, she and Luke were going to have a baby. It was the best birthday present she could ever receive. She had been so shocked by the test result that she had made them do another test before she would believe them. The results were conclusive; she was definitely pregnant.

Her back and head still hurt like the devil, but she didn't care. They had moved her to a regular room about ten minutes earlier. She had settled in within a moment, considering she only had one aching body dressed fashionably in a white-and-green-striped gown that was completely open in the back. Luke had been admiring the view, until he saw the bruise in the center of her back. Then he had grown silent and pensive until the nurses had left them alone. She had had a feeling she was about to listen to a major lecture and she really didn't think her head could take it, so she had begged Luke to go get the boys and her parents, who were waiting somewhere in the hospital to see her. She didn't want anything to spoil her mood, and no one realized more than she how lucky they had been to survive the tornado with only a few bumps and bruises to show for it.

Blessings seemed to come in twos.

"Mom!" Dalton's cry preceded him into the room. Someone had cleaned him up as best they could. He had two Band-Aids on one leg and one on the back of his hand. His smile took her breath away.

She held out her arms. "Come here and let me hug you." She glanced behind Dalton and spotted Blake. "You too, Blake." From her position, she counted four Band-Aids on her older son, but if it was possible, his smile was wider than Dalton's.

"Easy, boys, don't hug your Mom, let her hug

you." Luke stepped into the room, followed by her worried-looking parents.

She gave each of the boys a quick hug and big kiss and then patted the side of the bed. She wanted the boys close. Blake and Dalton climbed up onto the bed and sat. She had to smile at how cautious they were.

She smiled at her parents. "Mom, Dad, you didn't have to come. I'm fine."

Her mother hurried forward, gently kissed her cheek and then straightened the blanket. "Of course we had to come; you're our daughter." Her mother's voice was breaking on every other word and tears were slowly running down her face. "A tornado." A shudder shook her mother's body. "I can't imagine being caught in one of those."

"We weren't caught in one, we were hiding from one, right, boys?"

Blake and Dalton quickly nodded their heads in agreement. "It was big, Grandmom." Blake spread his arms, frowned and then tried to spread them farther. "Real big."

Dalton's head was still bobbing up and down. "It was scary, too."

"That's enough talk about tornadoes." Her father looked pale and shaken. "How are you feeling, honey?" He gruffly patted her shoulder and then brushed a kiss across her forehead.

Her father wasn't the emotional type and she was quite concerned by his appearance. "I'm fine, Dad." She pointed to the chair next to the bed. "Why don't you sit down and take a load off." Amazingly, her father sat.

"Luke's been busy running back and forth between the emergency room and the waiting room." Her mother's voice was slowly losing the trembling quality. The more she fussed about the room, the stronger she became.

Sue Ellen winked at her husband. "Yes, he's been *very busy* lately."

Luke wiggled his eyebrows at her and she couldn't contain the giggle tickling the back of her throat.

Her mother frowned at her. "Did they give you something for the pain?"

She shook her head. The pain wasn't that bad, and in her condition she really didn't want to be taking a bunch of pills that might harm the baby. She had a condition! She smiled at Luke, silently asking his permission to break the news.

Luke nodded his head.

"It's such a shame this had to happen, and on your birthday, too." Her mother was busy rearranging the trial-size personal hygiene products in the top drawer. "Luke had a party planned for you this evening."

She glanced back to her husband, who shrugged and looked a tad sheepish. "You did?"

"It was just your parents, the boys and a couple of ladies from the beauty shop. Your mom did the asking. I just volunteered our house."

"Wow, a party!" Blake bounced off the bed.

"Is there going to be cake?" Dalton stayed on the bed, but he was bouncing with excitement.

WIFE IN NAME ONLY   243

"I'm going to miss it." Luke was throwing her a party, and she wasn't even going to be there.

"I think under the circumstances we can postpone it until next weekend." Luke reached over and clamped a hand on Dalton's shoulder. "No bouncing."

"I guess I could freeze the cake." Her mother carefully unwrapped a new toothbrush and lined it up next to the toothpaste.

"I think if we're willing to share, the nurses will let us sneak it in here tonight."

"Wow, a party in the hospital!" Both of the boys' eyes lit up with excitement.

Her mother closed the drawer and moved the phone closer to the side of the bed. "This has been some day; first the tornado and now a party."

"It gets better." She gave her mother a warm smile. Her parents loved being stepgrandparents to the boys, but with Evelyn in town calling all the shots, it was a very difficult position to be in.

"How, Mom?" Dalton looked thrilled with the prospect of something better than a party.

She held her hand out to Luke, he took it and then she turned toward the boys. "It seems you two are going to have a baby sister or brother."

"You're pregnant!" Her mother's voice went back to being all trembly and teary as she reached for her husband's hand. "Is the baby all right?"

"The baby's fine." She patted her flat stomach and smiled at the boys. Both were staring at her, and then their father.

Blake's eyes narrowed slightly. "How come you're

not fat like Danny's mom? She's going to have a baby. Danny told me so, and she's real fat."

"I will be soon enough, Blake. As the baby grows, so will I." She squeezed Luke's hand. "I'm figuring by Christmas I'll be bigger than Santa."

Dalton's eyes grew wider. "Wow. I can't wait to tell everyone in my class."

"That you're going to have a baby brother or sister?" She was happy to see both of the boys seemed to be accepting the news rather well.

"No, I'm going to tell them about how the tornado gave my mom a baby."

Everyone in the room burst out laughing, except the boys. They both stared at the adults as if they had lost their minds. When she could control her mirth, she looked at Luke and said, "I'm leaving that one for you to handle."

"Thanks." Luke's deep chuckle told her that he didn't really mind too much.

"How about if I take the boys back to your house and get them changed, feed them dinner and then we can come back for some birthday cake?" Her mother was in her organizing mode. "Seems like we have a lot to celebrate tonight, and you could do with a real nightgown and robe."

Within minutes the room was once again empty, except for Luke. He collapsed into the chair her father had vacated and studied her face. "Are you sure you're up to cake tonight?"

"Wouldn't miss it for the world."

Before Luke could comment on that, the door was pushed open and a huge bouquet of flowers came wandering into the room. Evelyn was carrying the bouquet. A very upset Evelyn.

"Please, don't throw me out until I've had a chance to apologize." Evelyn's eyes were red and swollen from crying. She handed Luke the flowers. "These are for Sue Ellen."

Sue Ellen glanced at her husband. He looked as shocked as she did. Evelyn wanted to apologize, but whatever for? "Thank you, Evelyn. They're lovely." It was the largest bouquet she had ever seen.

"No, I'm the one who is thanking you, Sue Ellen. You saved the lives of my grandsons today." Evelyn sniffled into a tissue. "Words are totally inadequate to express my feelings, but they are all I have." Her fingers twisted the tissue into a tight ball. "Blake and Dalton are all I have. They could have died today, and it would have been my fault."

"I should have been paying closer attention to the weather." Sue Ellen felt her heart soften toward the older woman who had lost her only child. Her own hand went protectively to her stomach where her unborn baby lay.

"I acted terribly to you and Luke. I've been wrong all along. I never should have tried to take the boys away from Luke. I never should have interfered with how he was raising them. Blake and Dalton are wonderful boys, and he did and I'm sure will continue to do a wonderful job raising them." Evelyn pulled out another tissue and wiped at her eyes. "I should have made sure the boys were at my house when you told me you would be there. I shouldn't have been a half hour late, and I certainly shouldn't have threatened you."

"You threatened Sue Ellen?" Luke's expression, which had been softening, hardened.

"It was nothing, Luke." Evelyn's eyes pleaded with her for understanding. "It was just a bunch of nonsense, old rumors and such. I've completely forgotten what it was all about now anyway."

Sue Ellen understood, all right. Evelyn wasn't going to tell Luke the reason Ron had broken their engagement. Evelyn was offering her an olive branch, or maybe it was more like Evelyn begging her to accept a peace offering. Almost losing her grandsons today really seemed to have affected her. The woman was doing a complete turnabout. Life did manage to throw some curveballs every once in a while. Today's tornado could have taken a couple of players out of the game permanently.

Evelyn wasn't the only one counting her blessings. "It's all right, Evelyn. Luke knows."

"Luke knows what?" Her husband was staring from her to his ex-mother-in-law. He was still scowling.

"Evelyn found out why Ron broke our engagement. She thought I married you so that I could become a mother to your sons since I couldn't have children of my own." Her eyes were full of laughter as she looked at her husband.

Luke crossed his arms and tried to look duly upset. "Interesting."

"Sue Ellen's a wonderful mother, Luke." Evelyn stepped to the side of the bed. "At first I was upset

WIFE IN NAME ONLY 247

that she would try to take Tiffany's place in the boys' hearts. I know now she can't replace Tiffany by becoming their mother and loving them. Blake and Dalton need a mother, Luke. A good mother." Evelyn reached out and squeezed Sue Ellen's hand. "I can't think of a better one than Sue Ellen."

Luke slowly nodded. "You're right, Evelyn. I think I'll keep her."

"Stop teasing her, Luke." Sue Ellen reached out and patted Evelyn's hand. "It took a lot of courage and love to come in here and admit your fears, Evelyn. You will always be welcome in our home and in the boys' lives. You and Frank are family, for now and forever."

Tears were streaming down Evelyn's face. "Really?"

"Really." She moved over and made room for Evelyn to sit on the side of the bed. Today was indeed a day for miracles, so why fight it? Maybe she could create a little miracle of her own. "In fact, we are now facing an interesting dilemma that maybe you and Frank could help us out with."

"Anything." Evelyn wiped away the last of her tears, straightened her shoulders and looked ready to take on the world. "You name it and it's done."

"Well, since Luke's parents live so far away and we'll only be able to see them occasionally, when the work on the farm lets up enough for us to travel to Arizona, we're in need of a pair of surrogate grandparents."

Evelyn frowned. "I don't understand."

"Blake and Dalton will be getting a new baby brother or sister in about seven and a half months."

"You're pregnant!"

"Yes, and it's going to get awfully confusing, having one set of grandparents for Blake and Dalton and another set for this baby. So, we would be honored if you and Frank could find it in your hearts to accept another grandchild."

"After everything I did and said, you still want me to be a grandmother to your child?" The floodgates had been reopened and Evelyn was working her way into drowning them all.

"Yes, because underneath all those things I understood why you did it." Sue Ellen glanced at Luke to see how he was handling this, and he gave her a smile of encouragement. "We knew you were still grieving for Tiffany, and you were afraid you were losing the boys in the process. You will never lose the boys, Evelyn, never."

"She's right, Ev. You're family." Luke gave her a gentle smile. "You don't lose family."

Evelyn looked dazed. "I'm going to be a grandmother again?"

"Looks that way." Sue Ellen winked at her husband. "Of course, we're going to have to talk to you about spoiling the kids, but we'll do that some other time when I'm feeling more up to it."

"Oh, my. I should let you rest." Evelyn stood up and smoothed the wrinkles out of her skirt. "Is there anything I can get you?"

"No, but if you're quiet, you and Frank can sneak back in here about seven. Luke's bringing my birthday cake in and we're hoping to bribe a couple of nurses into letting us have a party."

"What did I just hear about bribing someone?" Sam, the sheriff, poked his head into the room and smiled. "Hey, if it ain't Pecos Bill! Wrestle any twisters lately?"

She stuck out her tongue at him. Sam was only a couple of years older than she and had lived on the street behind her parents' house when she was growing up. He had attacked her daily with a water gun and nicknamed her "squirt" because of her inability to outrun him. "Arrest anyone lately?"

"I can see you're feeling better, Squirt." Sam winked at her before handing Luke a brown paper bag and a set of keys. "Your truck is in the parking lot, and here's the package out of the glove compartment you wanted."

"Well, I've got to be going." Evelyn kissed Sue Ellen's cheek. "Thank you again, for everything."

She returned the gesture. "See you and Frank at seven."

"Come on, Evelyn, I'll walk you out." Sam winked at Luke. "See if you can keep that one"—he nodded toward the bed—"out of trouble."

Luke chuckled. "I'm trying."

Sue Ellen closed her eyes and listened to the silence. Silence was good.

"You want to rest?" Luke sat on the edge of the bed and brushed a lock of hair behind her ear. "I can come back later."

"No, don't go." She reached for his hand. "I don't want to be alone just yet."

"Okay, I'll stay." Luke threaded his fingers through hers. "How's the head?"

"The jackhammering has stopped. It's only a persistent hammering now." She glanced at the bag in his hand. "What's in the bag?"

"Your birthday present." Luke opened the bag and looked inside.

"When did you have time to get me a present?" She tried to see what was inside the bag, but the opening wasn't big enough.

"Last week." Luke smiled as he pulled out a small, beautifully wrapped box with a tiny bow stuck on top. The present was no bigger than a two-and-a-half-inch square. He carefully placed it in her hand. "Open it."

Her fingers trembled as she slowly undid the elegant foil wrapping. She just knew it was a jewelry box. Her heart pounded wildly as she opened the miniature package and saw a black velvet box inside. She bit her lip as she tipped the black box into the palm of her hand. She glanced at Luke.

He wasn't smiling now. He was intensely watching every move she made. She slowly opened the lid of the box and stared. A gorgeous diamond ring glittered back at her. Tears pooled in her eyes. "It's . . . it's . . ." Luke had gone out and gotten her an engagement ring!

"Will you marry me, Sue Ellen?" Luke took the box from her hand and removed the ring.

She blinked. "Marry you? I thought we were married!" She swiped at the tears rolling down her cheeks. "You already asked me to marry you."

"I asked you before for all the wrong reasons. I asked you to marry me to become the mother of my sons and to take care of us."

"And now?" She was having a hard time hearing him over the pounding of her heart.

"I'm asking now because I love you, and I don't want to spend another day of my life without telling you so."

"You love me?" Her hand covered her stomach as a new thought entered her mind. "It's not because of the baby, is it?"

"The receipt is in the bag, love. I bought the ring over a week ago. We didn't know about the baby until two hours ago." He held her hand captive and toyed with the ring without slipping it on her finger. "You still haven't answered the question, Sue Ellen. Will you marry me?"

She had been wrong. Blessings did come in threes. Luke loved her. "Yes!" She reached forward and brought his mouth closer to hers. "Just for the record, I want you to know one thing, dear husband of mine." Her mouth teased the corner of his.

"What's that?" came out like a groan instead of actual words.

"I love you too."

ABOUT THE AUTHOR

Marcia Evanick lives with her family in Pennsylvania. She is currently working on the second novel of her Wild Rose Trilogy, *Hand In Hand*, which will be published in September 2000. Marcia loves to hear from readers, and you may write to her c/o Zebra Books. Please include a self-addressed, stamped envelope if you wish a response.

BOOK YOUR PLACE ON OUR WEBSITE AND MAKE THE READING CONNECTION!

We've created a customized website just for our very special readers, where you can get the inside scoop on everything that's going on with Zebra, Pinnacle and Kensington books.

When you come online, you'll have the exciting opportunity to:

- View covers of upcoming books
- Read sample chapters
- Learn about our future publishing schedule (listed by publication month *and author*)
- Find out when your favorite authors will be visiting a city near you
- Search for and order backlist books from our online catalog
- Check out author bios and background information
- Send e-mail to your favorite authors
- Meet the Kensington staff online
- Join us in weekly chats with authors, readers and other guests
- Get writing guidelines
- AND MUCH MORE!

Visit our website at
http://www.zebrabooks.com

COMING IN JUNE FROM ZEBRA BOUQUET ROMANCES

#49 THE MEN OF SUGAR MOUNTAIN: TWO HEARTS
by Vivian Leiber
(0-8217-6623-6, $3.99) Kate left home in search of Mr. Right, and thought she'd found him in the big city. Now, broke and rejected by her blueblood husband, Kate is back home. She's determined to salvage her marriage, with some help from an unexpected ally—Sheriff Matt Skylar. Little does she know, the hunky lawman is planning to make her his wife!

#50 THE RIGHT CHOICE by Karen Drogin
(0-8217-6624-4, $3.99) Carly Wexler is planning her wedding the same way she has planned her life—perfectly, with no loose ends or real passion. Though her heart doesn't leap when she thinks of her fiancé, she's certain this union is for the best. Until she meets sexy Mike Novack, who is everything she's trying to avoid . . . hot, passionate, and forbidden.

#51 LOVE IN BLOOM by Michaila Callan
(0-8217-6625-2 $3.99) Seventeen years ago, model Eva Channing ran from the glamorous world of New York fashion to small town Texas where she could forget her passionate, doomed affair with photographer Carson Brandt. Today, Eva is content . . . until a magazine piece on former models brings Carson tumbling back into her life . . .

#52 WORTH THE WAIT by Kathryn Attalla
(0-8217-6626-0, $3.99) Abandoned to foster homes as a child, beautiful Charlie Lawson is steel and velvet on the outside but, on the inside, she's vulnerable and lonely. Even though she longs for romance, Charlie decided never to give anyone the chance to hurt her . . . until sexy, compassionate Damian Westfield makes her believe in love again.

Call toll free **1-888-345-BOOK** to order by phone or use this coupon to order by mail.
Name_____
Address_____
City_____ State _____ Zip _____
Please send me the books I have checked above.
I am enclosing $_____
Plus postage and handling* $_____
Sales tax (in NY and TN) $_____
Total amount enclosed $_____
*Add *$2.50* for the first book and *$.50* for each additional book.
Send check or money order (no cash or CODs) to:
Kensington Publishing Corp. Dept. C.O., 850 Third Avenue, New York, NY 10022.
Prices and numbers subject to change without notice. Valid only in the U.S.
All books will be available *6/1/00*. All orders subject to availability.
Visit our website at **www.kensingtonbooks.com**.

**LOVE STORIES YOU'LL NEVER FORGET...
IN ONE FABULOUSLY ROMANTIC NEW LINE**

BALLAD ROMANCES

Each month, four new historical series by both beloved and brand-new authors will begin or continue. These linked stories will introduce proud families, reveal ancient promises, and take us down the path to true love. In Ballad, the romance doesn't end with just one book...

COMING IN JULY
EVERYWHERE BOOKS ARE SOLD

The Wishing Well Trilogy:
CATHERINE'S WISH, by Joy Reed.
When a woman looks into the wishing well at Honeywell House, she sees the face of the man she will marry.

Titled Texans:
NOBILITY RANCH, by Cynthia Sterling
The three sons of an English earl come to Texas in the 1880s to find their fortunes... and lose their hearts.

Irish Blessing:
REILLY'S LAW, by Elizabeth Keys
For an Irish family of shipbuilders, an ancient gift allows them to "see" their perfect mate.

The Acadians:
EMILIE, by Cherie Claire
The daughters of an Acadian exile struggle for new lives in 18th-century Louisiana.